Drift

A novel

Craig Rodgers

ISBN: 978-1-0881-0764-5

Published by Death of Print

deathofprint.press

Cover design by Alan Good and Craig Rodgers

Typeset by Alan Good in Baskerville

Praise for *Drift*

Drift captures the tedious terror—and terrifying tedium—of contemporary life like nothing I've seen. Craig Rodgers performs the neatest of tricks, sending European-style ennui (think Sartre and Camus) on a thrill ride through a uniquely American hell.

—Jennifer Wortman,
author of T*his. This. This. Is. Love. Love. Love.*

With *Drift*, Craig Rodgers cements himself as a writer of considerable talent and limitless creative ambition. Following the exploits of a self-described piece of human spam, the novel trawls the liminal spaces and empty corridors of the often crappy and occasionally edifying experience of being alive in America. Rodgers's prose is spare, comedic, and deployed with a craftsman's attention to detail. Paced perfectly, *Drift* is the literary page-turner of the year.

—Kyle Seibel, author of Hey *You Assholes*

Drift is a potent literary moonshine that distills the existential milieux of McCarthy and the post-modern dysphoria of Bachman.

—Alan ten-Hoeve,
author of *Notes from a Wood-Paneled Basement*

Drift by Craig Rodgers reads in the author's signature style — the familiar charm of characters from another time somehow thrust into a world they don't belong to, an initially-pleasant vintage dancing toward something faintly macabre. In this case, it is Charlie, a Bible salesman who, in the slow process of losing himself, embarks on a darkly-tinged trip both literally and through his own consciousness. Bleak, twisting, and satisfying, Rodgers seamlessly curates the details of each moment, weaving them together into a knot you'll want to follow to the end.

—Tiffany M Storrs, Editor in chief, Roi Fainèant Press

In *Drift*, the prose escalates with a relentless force, each step drawing you away from the grounded world you thought you were witnessing. Narration is as unyielding as steel, thrusting you into a realm where the boundaries between reality and illusion blur and shift like mirages on the horizon. Craig's narration is a force of nature, plunging you headlong into a world where the divine and the profane are locked in a dance of mundanity. The language is crisp, dragging you by the shirt collar through the purgatorial landscape of the soul.

—Jake Blackwood, cyberwriter

Craig Rodgers writes with unhinged force. This book, these characters are here for all the honest world to feel. It's blood and snot, it's a lonely bathroom light. No joke, *Drift* is one to cherish. Let it stick to the ribs. Take the ride.

—Adam Van Winkle, author of *Dylan Quick is a Dairy Queen Don Quixote* and EIC of Cowboy Jamboree Press

A rare gift. Craig Rodgers is a master of mood and style. Each chapter resonates, stays with you like a velvet ghost.

—Autumn Christian, author of *Girl Like a Bomb*

A bit of DeLillo's *Americana* and a dash of Johnson's *Angels*, *Drift* reads like a long lost underground American novel. The prose is like watching a femme fatale slowly strip off her clothes but you can never quite see her face. Decadent, surreal, memorable.

—Tex Gresham,
writer/director of *Mustard,* author of *Sunflower*

A NOTE

A goal, among others, for this book is that a writer / director of great talent will see in its strengths the makings of a fine film and one day its screen adaptation will be two thumbs downed by eerie deepfakes of Siskel and Ebert.

Craig Rodgers
2/27/2023

1.

There is a roar from underneath, an unending rush of some great force that will not be ignored. These old roads are just that way, hard-packed blacktop shrieking at the passage of beasts above, a road noise so loud that the tinny bars of some saccharine pop classic playing out of cheap door speakers is almost lost completely.

His name is Charlie, a tag which is stamped in affirmative bold on the card he's supposed to hand with a dimple-filled smile to each new client. A stack of these cards rattles around the glove box, a rubber band holding them together as its elastic slowly dries and its purpose slips away. *Sales*, says the card with a lackadaisical flair for its own ambiguity. A bible sits on the dash vibrating to the beat of the pavement's roar. The cover is made up of the same intense blue as the sky.

In the distance hangs the hazy suggestion of a city, a prefab dream full of right angles existing on the horizon. Between this place and that is a vast emptiness cleaved by a single line whose unfolding is more or less straight while to each side washes a tide of yellow grassland and here and there the awkward bends of a sleeping tree. No one passes in the opposing lane. Any traveler found in these miles of desolation has but one destination before them.

His tie is loose but still tied, the slack bulge of knot still intact. He paid a motel maid five dollars to tie it for him. The knot always looks wrong when he does it himself.

2.

A slack face is what he wears until the very moment the door opens before him, letting free the heady aroma of perfume and life to waft with lazy abandon into the scentless second-floor hallway of a modern, dull complex of office suites. A smile appears with professional timing as he turns his face upon the prosaic figure of a young woman standing in the doorway. Her disinterest sways and falls away as she finds Charlie in her way. She stops short, one foot raised and dropped before the step it was about to take.

"I knocked," he says without real commitment. Maybe he did knock, maybe it's true.

She looks down the hallway, first one way and then the other. A man several doors down stands paused outside another suite, utterly engrossed in the banal particulars of some paperwork in hand.

Charlie is already talking as he slips past the woman.

"I brought along a few samples. Same stuff we have on the website, but, come on. You can't really get a sense of what you're buying that way. A person wants to smell the ink. They want to feel what they're getting."

She shuts the door and follows him through another doorway. Inner office. He remains standing, lounging against a desk with one hand and letting the sample case dangle from the other as the woman rounds the stained oak frame, putting the bulk of the workstation between Charlie and herself.

"You're early."

She says it with a casual bite, not quite accusatory and not quite not.

"I'm punctual," he counters, all dimples and ease.

They talk, him going on about books, her talking price versus volume. She brings up the website, he cranes so he can see. She pivots the monitor, he comes around the desk. He points out items with a pinky, drawing attention to what he wants her to want. He uses words like *leather* and *guarantee*. He tells her to enter his name in the box on the right when she places her order. A discount, he says.

His hand moves slow as he retrieves the sky-blue book from the sample case. He lets her touch it, lets her run a hand over the contoured surface, half a smile pulling at the corner of her mouth.

He has her.

She handles the business for three churches in town. The order she makes covers all three. He leaves her with a demure tome the color of mud. Her eyes are on the book she holds as he slips the blue sample back into the case. She isn't looking as he nods and smiles and is already gone.

The smile is erased as the door closes at his back. He looks out of a slack face, giving away nothing. The man at the end of the hall looks up from the paperwork in his hand. He nods in vague human connection. Charlie walks in the other direction.

———

He doesn't know the name of the town. This morning he knew, or this morning he'd read it, let his eyes linger long enough to commit it to the scant strip of memory he knew himself willing to part with as the day progressed, and there, now, the name of the town is gone, another place he's already left behind even if the rest of him is still hours from that fated parting.

Gravel crunches under worn tires as he wheels into the motel lot. He parks alongside a beast of a car. Long black hardtop, whitewalls unsullied. '50s, maybe. An ancient thing. The company car from which Charlie emerges is a blight, a dull thing with every edge rounded and bland and utterly without heart. He pauses on loose ground, a hunger swelling, part of him taken by the thought of crossing the street to a chain eatery full of unbound ties and toothy carnivores while some other part of him wishes he'd already gotten a room, was now asleep, was not here at this moment having to make this decision. Somewhere nearby windows shake in their frames under the rumbling passage of an unseen train.

He takes the sample case along as tired feet drag him across the street, not looking this way or that for the aggressive surge of looming traffic, but no traffic comes to prevent this passing.

Sound rises with the door's opening. A muted yellow world inside, the glow of dim lights and the hovering scent of meat and grease crowd the senses, a palpable presence that coats. A hostess presents a manic grin and wide, haunting eyes that Charlie looks too long into, unable to turn from the unrelenting draw they offer without shame.

"Just one?"

She says it without malice but he flinches just the same.

"Smoking," and as an afterthought, "please."

The grin persists and those haunting eyes do not blink.

"We no longer have a smoking section in the dining area but you're welcome to smoke on the patio."

A man with sleeves rolled to elbows cuts at a burned slab of meat at the single table outside. On his head is a bowler hat, its cloth dented, lived in. Charlie doesn't look at a menu, mumbles the first thing that comes to mind.

"Reuben sandwich."

Her grin does not change.

"I'm the hostess."

He stares blankly back.

"I'm not your waitress."

If there is more he does not hear. The bag in his hand is an albatross that pulls at his arm as he makes his slow way, weaving between tables and the lives of strangers existing and seething in loud jubilation in the path of every away. Writhing mass of life. Utensils scrape across glassware and mouths cackle. As Charlie breaks through the other side the door is there, the world just on the other side. A waitress passes, smiles a sane smile. She does not belong here. He orders his sandwich, points to the table outside, more words caught somewhere between himself and his mouth but she understands and nods and is soon gone to make things happen. He takes a seat at the patio table.

The man with the steak puts out a gloved hand, his palm turned up in vague acquiescence, an acceptance that this is happening. Sit, it says, but Charlie already has. The gloves have no fingers, their cloth cut away and the remains frayed. A dusty relic, this man. The lump of a cigarette pack stands out in the pocket of a waistcoat. Shrewd eyes of a carnival barker, some dustbowl urchin now wandered in out of the past. The man goes back to cutting, the knife going through line after line of the meat.

"Put you at the kids table, too," says the man. He takes no bites between cuts, taking care to slice each piece and move it aside as he goes to the next, preparing but not eating. "There's no ashtray."

A lit cigarette sits balanced on the lip of an empty coffee cup. The lightest touch from wind would upset its delicate state, but the day is still, paused in waiting.

"You a local?"

"I don't want to buy anything. I don't want anything."

The man laughs. "Just conversation. Just making conversation," he says.

Charlie shakes his head. The man finishes his cuts and places the knife on a napkin.

"Me neither. What do you do?"

"Sales. Traveling sales. I facilitate purchases while acting as the national face of the company."

The man takes a fork in hand but doesn't eat.

"That sounds like a prepared statement."

"It is," says Charlie. "I go around reminding people that every few years they need to replace books handled by grubby hands on a regular basis. Sounds better the other way."

The man takes a bite of the charred meat. His face is neutral, placid. Teeth grind in silence. He swallows and speaks.

"Is it a good job?"

"It's an easy job. I meet the appointments someone else makes and I help people buy what they already want. I drive a lot. I drive all the time."

The man goes on eating, forking small bites of meat and chewing, one after another without comment for minutes. If he feels an awkwardness in the quiet he leaves before him it does not show. The restaurant's side door opens and lets loose the banging cacophony of its inner horror. The confused patron in the doorway looks around, brow curling over brooding eyes. The madness at its back pulls that formless ape back inside and slams the door in its wake.

The man stops eating halfway through the steak. He sets the fork next to the knife. Napkin soaks grease. The weak blue of the table can be seen underneath. He's slow to look up, speaking before he does.

"Is that satisfying work?"

"No."

A waitress appears, a different face from the last, this one a stranger. She brings Charlie's sandwich and if she speaks it is a perfunctory friendliness. The man in the bowler smokes in silence and Charlie eats and soon it is clear there is nothing more to say. The man nods and only that as he stands and turns and walks on thick-soled boots around a corner and away. It is only now that Charlie realizes the man said nothing about himself.

A pack of cigarettes sits nestled in a pocket of the suit coat that hangs limp on Charlie's sunken frame. He thinks about smoking but doesn't. He puts a ten-dollar bill under the cup of ashes, then puts down another two singles. He doesn't wait for the check.

The long black classic is gone when he crosses back to the motel. The lot is half empty, slots filled at random and no two alike. A bag with essentials is forgotten, toiletries and clothes and the all-purpose baubles of everyday life left behind in the company car as he passes. His one clasped bag, the sample case, comes along to the motel check-in.

He pays for the room with a company card without saying two words to the clerk at the front desk. The clerk doesn't notice. A television plays a talk show in a foreign language, the sets decked out in vibrant '70s chic. A host shows teeth and nods a lot. He moves his hands when he talks. The topic is impossible to guess. A current events piece about a clown. Charlie takes the room key.

The motel room smells like someone's dinner, a nameless spice floating on the air in a lusty heat. Cooking in the next room, or not. Maybe a room further down, somewhere distant, a place only connected through the labyrinthine meanderings of a duct system. Charlie doesn't care. He drops the sample case on the floor and falls to the bed. He's already asleep when his phone begins to ring.

3.

The sun is a broken thing, slices of shine clawing their way through the slats of dusty blinds. The perpetual rise and fall of white noise is the snake of passing cars on the highway three blocks over. Charlie's phone sits on the nightstand. A light blinks on its front from time to time. Once, twice a minute. He reaches for it before the blur of sleep leaves his eyes and he regains his place in the world.

Missed calls but no messages. He dials in a morning fog. It picks up on the second ring.

"Office. This is Jess."

Her voice is a pleasant thing, dancing up and down on all the right words. She tells him she's updated his itinerary, that he should check his email. No, there's no message from upstairs, she says. She says the office is warm.

He isn't listening. He nods into the phone as he watches the flashing passage of cars on the highway glimpsed in the cracks between buildings like the flicker of film as it makes its mad run though a projector. A million lives on their way to somewhere. Just passing by.

He says thank you as he hangs up. It's 9 a.m.

———

The tie is wrong. A disfigured lump, a tumor with mismatched ends hanging from its imperfect knot. Charlie fusses with its fickle ends as he waits, untying and retying. It does no good.

The waiting room smells like a flower, something he should know the name of but doesn't. A familiar smell. He breathes it in and holds, trying to remember, but there is nothing there. A woman looks at a computer screen. Maybe a secretary. She takes his name and has him sit and she looks at the unchanging page of a social networking site as she waits for the phone to ring, a client to come, something to change. Charlie pulls at his tie.

Two hours of white knuckles among the dizzying fray of impromptu midday traffic leads to this place and this moment, untold variables aligning to allow now to transpire. He watches the secretary in the glow of her monitor. She reads things she's read once, twice already, lips moving with the words so that for fractions of a thought there appears a glimpse into that mouth, that dark place where those whispered words are born. He sees in her the ephemeral trace of all loves that a ghost of memory touches, the pang of the past that means something underneath the skin. He sees hot summers and movie theaters and grass more green than grass could possibly be and he loses himself for just a second and no more in the velvet fall of that memory's hold. He watches her smile at something she sees and he doesn't ask her name, knowing that to do so is to open an infinite list of possibly maybes, finding himself in all of the futures in which he cannot be. Married, kids and a dog, a house like every other on the block, on every block, a universe of such houses squeezed from the same mold birthed by a God so easily amused. Nine-to-fiving his way through years in a farm of cubicles manned by sane commuters and rational dressers with chairs that glide on mechanisms well oiled by an assistant or intern whose sole purpose in this life is to retain the silent integrity of office chairs. Being in this town for another day. Each of these futures want for a valor he cannot will himself to muster.

"Is that a potpourri?"

She blinks before turning, the dry rush of his question shaking her out of her own unfathomable reverie as she remembers she is not alone in the room.

"I'm sorry?"

He gestures at nothing, pointing a hand around the room in ambiguous salute.

"Air freshener or something?"

A shrug is all that comes for a moment and maybe it is all she intends to offer, but she finds herself giving more regardless.

"She got flowers," she says, hooking a thumb over her shoulder at the door to an inner office. "Her boyfriend took her to lunch."

"Your boss."

"What?"

"She's still at lunch. Your boss is."

Her stare says yes, says it's obvious, that he should've picked up on this on his own. It says that he is a fool for waiting this long.

"What am I here for?"

She looks around for nothing in particular, a moment's busying gesture to deflate the implication before she offers a placating response.

"She should be back."

Charlie picks up his bag, his professional smile growing across his placid face like some eager pox overtaking all it touches. He could explain to this vapid pretty thing what there is to know, what icons to click and what order to place, a quick re-up. The same few mundane actions her employer will no doubt undertake today or tomorrow. Someday. He could tell her where to put his name so that he gets a little extra in his check and they get a little extra off the bill, but he doesn't. That smile overtakes all, an unstoppable thing. Soon he says thank you and leans ponderously forward, breathing in her air and smiling that smile as she first leans away but soon she too leans in, taken by the intrigue of this departure from the tap of keys and the glow of a screen and the ringing of phones and all the banal tedium that until this moment loomed unflinching over her days. And she's smiling, for him she's smiling the same smile she gave up to that glow of the infinite only minutes before.

"What's your name?" he asks.

———

He wakes from a dream he does not remember. He reaches out as it recedes in mind but the wispy tendrils of ephemera evaporate, leaving behind only a formless disquiet. The TV is on. A movie plays, something old, all the actors moving with a stiff pride. He doesn't look at the screen and its light plays on the walls behind his thoughts. He takes hold of the remote but only sits there with it, hand on lap.

She breathes quietly, a creature afraid of waking even herself. An arm hangs off the side of the bed, a leg doing almost the same, her appendages only pale ropes dangling unknowing over the abyss. He wants to wake her and for only this moment bask in the perfection which only strangers can achieve. He turns off the television and the world disappears.

He dresses in the dark, looping tie around neck but not pulling ends taut. The whoosh of cars rattles windows, goes on unending in the world outside. Even at this hour that world churns without rest. A shirt is untucked and belt fastened loose. Hair hangs in exasperated arcs, baffled at its own placement. He turns in a circle in the dark. Surveying. He has been in this room a thousand times before in dozens of cities and it is always the same even as it isn't.

There is a painting on one wall. A sad thing sold in a garage sale or found by a dumpster. Quick brushstrokes make a field of some grain. Shaded texture in the background barely shows; a home or barn, some kind of structure. A faint thing, unimportant to this field. The field is an empty place.

A notepad on the dresser gives the name of the motel chain across the top of the page. Half-used stationary. Charlie opens the door to let in the touch of light. He wants to leave a note, to leave behind something more than fleeting moments, a last line of substance to connect with a memory that would surely fade into the background of life if left on its own. He wants to be remembered, but the notepad is still blank as he steps into the night, the door closing on silent hinges as he goes.

———

The willful rush of the road strives to eclipse the phone's shrill call. Charlie ignores the first ring and the second but eventually he gives in. His foot eases back on the gas, slowing the car by five miles an hour or ten. He straightens in his seat and clears his throat. He presses the call button.

"I'm up."

"Office calling."

"I know."

"You're up?"

"Why are you calling me this early?"

Keys tap on the other end of the line, a chorus of soft strokes that pleases the ear. She averages sixty words per minute. She's still typing as she speaks her reply.

"You check the itinerary this morning?"

"I'm booked through next week and I've got the conference coming. Are you putting me on a plane?"

"It's not that."

"Then there's no room for more."

For a moment there is only the sound of her typing. When she speaks her words are plucked from a bottomless pool of patience.

"Are you done?" she asks.

"Okay."

"Today's guy pushed back a few hours."

Charlie clears his throat again, not turning from the phone as he does. The noise becomes a single word.

"Why?"

"He's a big client, Charlie."

"What's his deal?"

"Fuck should I know? He's double-booked, something."

Charlie takes the phone from his ear. He looks at it but there is nothing there that changes the moment. He drives too fast and the dawn remains somewhere beyond the horizon.

"What time do I meet him?"

"Check the itinerary."

"Jess, I've had maybe two hours sleep and I'm gonna be driving at least into mid-morning, and that's if I don't hit heavy traffic, which I'm going to. How long am I awake today?"

It goes on that way, him asking questions he could answer himself, her asking questions that don't matter, just talking, each saying things to be saying them, to hear another voice besides their own. She doesn't ask why he hasn't slept. He doesn't ask why she's in the office at this hour. The comforting prattle dwindles to a thread and soon is only air and quiet. He hangs up because he doesn't know what else to say. It's almost 4 a.m.

———

Engine hums, a fay idle burning away fuel that should matter but doesn't. A man on the radio talks about his life between songs. Half-formed jokes and too much laughing. Charlie isn't listening, doesn't hear. He chews his slow way through bites of a gas station sandwich. Wet bread, gray meat, a mess soaked in salt. The sun waits high overhead watching the indifferent march of hours go by.

Cars line the street, a fence of parked hulks encircling a city block dominated by a single bleak structure. A courthouse, or it was at one time, a century ago maybe, this waxen facade with spires climbing from predictable placings. Bright grass covers a well tended lawn all around. Twenty-somethings eat vegan lunches out of vintage lunchboxes or they toss objects, frisbees or more arcane finds. The scene could be stopped, paused only a moment, and sold to passersby as a postcard in a giftshop by the roadside.

Shrieking brakes cut through the pleasing midday thrum as a bus pulls to a curb. A sigh opens the door. People step onto the street; townies and students, an elderly man with a box under one pale, papery arm. A game or maybe shoes. Among the few stateless drifters walks a man in a waistcoat. A gloved hand holds a bowler hat that he looks at for long seconds before placing its dented form upon his head. Charlie mutters a word to himself but even he does not know what he's said. The bus waits to see what happens. Doors close but still it stays, its reluctance a palpable thing, a presence all its own. A minute goes by and the bus pulls away.

A song goes by on the radio, maudlin lyrics sung by a voice that misses the point. It plays and ends and the man still stands at the curb. He looks into the sky, into the sun, ignorant of the ruthless presence returning that look. Retinas should wither in ruin and decay but don't, only stare up in defiance. Only as clouds pass and the day grows steeped in shade does he turn away, this goon in outdated garb. Shrewd eyes search the streets, the faces crowded there, eyes capturing moments in mind, stealing fragments of time and storing them away in cold memory. Satisfied with all he's found, he walks away along sidewalk ringing the block until the grim edifice of that primordial house of judgment snatches all evidence of his ever being. The song ends and in its place there rises a long moment of dead air.

———

It's a black spot, a place where light ends. Streetlamps trail off in every direction away from this place, but the light stops at its edge and inside this pocket void is laid acres of macadam marked by the slanting division of a thousand white lines. The building beyond the lot is a church, its face squared and unadorned. A warehouse for religion. The lot is inhabited by only the darkness and somewhere at its center a flickering warmth.

Headlights wash over the barren landscape, illuminating little as they make their way. He stops the car well short of the fire and the barrel and the man that stands just outside of that glow, a hovering face and sometimes hands that from time to time toss a featureless object into the contained conflagration. That face floats atop a white stripe in the dark. The collar of a priest. Charlie stays where he sits for a minute, the sound of some rock classic working its way through speakers. He lets the music work its way down to nothing as the man beyond the barrel drops objects into his drum of hell. The fire does not change as objects go in, or if it does it is a change beneath notice, a private thing known only to the fire and its untiring attendant. Charlie steps out of the car.

The priest watches this interloper's approach. Measured step across an acre of lot.

"You're not the other guy."

Charlie puts on his salesman's mask, responds with a single vague syllable.

"Yeah?"

"The last guy to come through."

The last sales call here was five years ago, maybe more. Charlie shrugs.

"I used to stick close to the office."

The priest nods.

"Well," he says. He tosses an object into the fire. "What have you got for me?"

Charlie looks at his side, around at his feet and at his empty hand. He turns at the waist to look back at the car. Mouth agape in idiot pose.

"My samples."

The priest nods again.

"Don't bother. It's pretty straightforward."

At his back are boxes, amorphous growths in the dark that gain only a semblance of shape as he steps to one or another, his presence adding to their own by some unutterable means beyond realm of measure. He leans down but finds nothing there, pushes the box away where it is taken by the darkness. He moves to another box and grabs more objects, these stacked flush with the box's brim.

Charlie watches the priest toss a bible into the fire.

"Why?"

"Why what?"

"Why burn them?"

The priest pauses with a book held out, not yet tossed away, still able to be saved.

"Speak your mind," says the priest.

"It's a waste. They're perfectly fine."

"I'm buying new ones. From you. Circle of life."

Charlie looks back at the car again but there is no answer there to find. The priest speaks again.

"You look exhausted."

Charlie shrugs.

"I dream a lot."

The priest laughs and tosses a bible into the fire. Charlie points an unsteady hand at the car and makes a feeble grasp for the reason he's here.

"We have a variety of options for our bigger clients."

The priest kicks an empty box into the void.

"Enough, enough, enough. I'll place my order. I'll go on the website. You get a commission bump?"

"If you put my name in the space."

"Your name, yeah. I'll place my order. Tomorrow, scout's honor. Fair enough?"

Charlie waits, and then he doesn't.

"So what, then?"

"What?"

"We're just standing here."

The priest holds out a book, an offering held above the fire.

"You want to do one?"

Hands go up and Charlie leans away in unnecessary dodge. The priest tosses the book into the barrel. A sincere reluctance keeps those hands in air, only time allowing them to make their slow way down to eventually rest in worn pockets of threadbare slacks. He watches the flames and he watches the priest, the wandering fire coloring skin a muddy orange. Silence plays out, but not a true silence, only the faded quiet of existence between bouts of violent noise. The crackle of flame and its enduring meal. Cars somewhere, always. Something pops in the fire.

"Why not burn the boxes?"

"I can use the boxes."

The priest gives another book to the fire.

———

Beyond the city a dwindling string of sun still burns. Vestiges of an already lost day die away on the horizon, a fading pink to the west and a nameless void to its reverse, that creeping advance of the inevitable to the east. Out here in the place between places land rises and falls as only a suggestion of hills in the dark, patches here and there more substantial creating a landscape more felt than seen. Further into the fields run trees and beyond them could be anything. Charlie sits on the cement guard of a bridge turnaround which runs above the interstate. The company car sits parked on the shoulder below. The engine ticks from use. Cars pass beneath Charlie's dangling feet from time to time, a splash of headlights reawakening the world for only the space that exists in front of their oncoming sprint. The blacktop accepts this fleeting incursion, opening before these steel transients and then closing once more, the red dot of diminishing taillights a last haunting remnant long after the beast to which they belong has gone, and soon time and distance take those feeble red lights as well. Over and over it occurs, each car's passage the same as that of all who come before. The last line of day on the western horizon falls to that same inevitable end.

Somewhere in that place beyond the trees the ground quakes under the passage of an unseen train. After a time its horn screams in the night marking the relentless approach to one city or another.

———

Charlie wakes in the car. Arms shoot through jacket sleeves worn backwards like a bib or blanket. He pulls it off and throws it aside. The sun is off somewhere in the east beyond the bridge turnaround under which Charlie is parked and the morning is a settled cold. Graffiti along the walls of this concrete cave tries and fails to share some arcane communication. The meticulous block lettering employed exclusively by the insane. *SAVE YOURSELF.* Their story is vague but compelling, a sincere desperation etched onto the world in absence of all meaning. A thing impossible to leave behind.

Coins rattle in console cup holder under the vibrating phone's ring. A cord trails out, is plugged into the hole where a lighter would be in a real car. The number displayed on the phone's glowing face is the office line. He closes his eyes and the ringing stops. It's just shy of 7 a.m.

4.

The sound is there, that unending rush of air and road and time moving ever past in the sprawled wasteland between one place and another, that emptiness broken only by road signs denoting forgotten locales called by ominous names. It consumes, that sound does, entering and expanding, making its home in ears and ballooning until brain and soul and man have all been enveloped in its maddening cocoon. It lords in that vacuum between places, a thing unmoved by the voices and smacks and the vicious noise which inhabits worlds peopled by the wandering denizens who name cities home. Such civilian logic has no place here in the barren province of that relentless sigh.

The pedal is pressed too hard and the car thrusts too fast into the world beyond itself as Charlie leans in and forces his reckless way into the future and the appointment that waits for him there. Hunger squeezes his middle, a wanting there left untended, and he wonders if there remains time enough for something, a quick bite in some nameless dive along the highway, even as he knows that scant spare time has already been displaced.

Cityscape looms and soon is everywhere, a presence swallowing all who come too close. He weaves his determined way through streets he doesn't know but quickly learns as he zeroes in on this morning's pursuit. Lights change from red to green at his approach, each occurrence beckoning him onward ever deeper into that writhing hive. The radio is on but turned low. Vast signs stretch over streets to form crude tunnels in whose shaded interiors trespass mortal wanderers. One sign stands beside and not over the expanse of street, a mammoth billboard seemingly related to none of its squalid surroundings and decorated by its single cryptic word. *JESUS*. Vultures line telephone poles, one after another looking down on the world and somewhere nearby something is dead.

Miles and minutes bring Charlie on time to his destination. The jingle of keys and death rattle of engine mark his arrived presence and the car locks and he's off. He enters a small church house, a single room and little more with pews waxed by a loving hand facing a plank dais where a man may stand and speak. An older man sits in one pew near the back, street clothes but professional in the squared shoulders and the jaw of a soldier. He laughs at a joke that Charlie barely tells, friendly greetings they've both heard before. The man is not a priest, is someone's assistant, a honed jocularity wrapped as carapace on top of a steely demeanor. He returns jokes as they come and swirls in a guise of ease through the rote exchange of quid pro quo. Hunger returns and stays, a churning want that knots and pulls as it gains traction, expands its hold in Charlie's middle. Charlie eyes the steel underneath conversation but ignores its unneeded presence. Standard details play out; name in website, discount for goods, all the points the list says need said. The man is bored with Charlie. Charlie is bored with himself. Quick smiles and easy sell and handshake and done.

The street has changed in the twenty minutes, thirty minutes in which it has pined for Charlie's return. The harsh white of new sun has become the tedious omnipresence of full day. A surge and spill of humanity onto cracked pavement streets has coalesced into a thick, slow sludge of progress between any two points and this seething mass of body and car congestion yanks thought of a smooth ride to a reputable steak joint from the reaching grasp of possibility. He stews for seconds, not thinking to search but only fuming at the injustice of it all. Hunger cramps again. Walking occurs as a feasible option only after long minutes have passed.

Two blocks over the cloying ghost of a bread scent overtakes the acrid choke of exhaust. Parked at the curb is a long black hardtop, old but pristine, whitewalls bright with daytime alacrity. A door leads out of the world and into that warm bread smell and he finds himself in a sunlit eatery like any he's been to, one he's maybe been to once or a hundred times but whose memory he's each time left behind once returned to the world.

He sits at a long bar running the length of the room and back again with checkers and staff manning an alley in between and he orders from a paper menu handed his way by a skeletal apparition who may work here or may just be trapped, unable to leave this luminous, hallowed place. He does not know what he orders, only that he reads from the menu the first thing that eyes land upon and he knows that whatever comes he will eat and love. A waitress chews gum and sets a plate in front of Charlie and he eats half before he thinks to slow, for manners or for public observance of some hint of normalcy or just for the sake of the sane approach to yet another meal. Eggs and coffee and toasted bread baked here in this place. The next bite is slow and the taste is there, that soft warmth and a sweetness and butter and he closes his eyes as even the slightest touch of crisp scorch on that bread is a religious experience.

Across the room, across the island bar and its alley of bees working in its middle, across the way there sits a large man drinking black oil coffee, swirls of its potency displayed on that slick surface for all the world to see. The man wears the coat of a preacher or undertaker, the frock coat of a man of another time and place. This man's pale face is oval, long, a misshapen thing with eyes that see too much. He leans into conversation with a smaller man, a muscled thing in a waistcoat and white collar with sleeves rolled to elbows and ratty fingerless gloves splayed out on the bar's Formica countertop. On his head is a dented bowler. The goon laughs at something the pale man with the oval face says. The pale man does not laugh with him.

"More coffee?"

Waitress with gum. She smiles the smile of the strong of heart or the oblivious. She refills Charlie's cup without waiting for an answer or she knows the answer before she's asked. Maybe he whispers a soft kiss of a yes as she pours, hoping she recognizes his answer, hoping she knows she has not been ignored. She moves on and so does he.

———

Pumping gas along a line of high-octane pillars. Numbers roll and he doesn't follow their march, doesn't care about the sum total of his debt accrued. He watches the street as he waits. A line of vans and trucks passes by among the congealed crawl of daytime cars, vibrant murals painted on the flanks of each; clowns and animals, exotic and some more mundane, even the dull lambs and one oversized mouse with its blank eyes strain at the edges of that mural, aching to burst their way into this other world.

He waits in line like anyone would. A girl, twenties, stands at the counter buying chips, buying water flavored how someone somewhere thinks lemon tastes. Her pants hang too low, her belt loops empty. Underwear shows. A parent is mortified in some other life. She pays in wadded bills she pulls from a pocket and she's gone. Charlie pays with the company card he pulls from his coat's inner pocket. He adds on cigarettes and a drink, some kind of water that tastes like water. He briefly wonders if someone at the office will care about the pittance these extra items come to as he hands over the card. He says thank you to the cashier.

———

He rinses his mouth with water. His watch ticks off several seconds as he checks it and checks it again. The day hums its presence at his back, all the moving things moving. A horn squawks a meaningless noise. He swishes and spits and takes another drink. The taste of cigarettes remains on his tongue and in his clothes. He pushes through the door and into the air-conditioned interior of a turn-of-the-century church.

Tall ceilings echo the footfalls which bring him through the empty room. Midsize congregation, maybe a few hundred on a good day. Today there is only Charlie and the weak patter of his advancing step. The shined lacquer used to buff each empty bench a day ago or maybe two is a cloying sweetness in the room. Breeze blows from unseen ducts and the heat of the day is shut outside.

He checks his watch again. A voice speaks.

"Everybody's gone."

He only now sees her sitting two benches from the back, in among the emptiness, another stranger he may have met one or a hundred times before. Her words sit alone a moment, waiting to be returned.

"I'm sorry?"

He knows it's the wrong response even as he says it. He checks his watch again, not for the time but only for cover, something to hide behind.

"They're at the funeral."

He takes a step back, away from her or away from her words. He looks around the room, its ceiling somewhere high above. The light is a serene flood coming from everywhere and the air is thin, the air of a mountaintop, each breath a reach to fill lung with that too-rich air. Everything in the room is bigger than itself, the walls too far apart and these few breathing things must do all they can to fill that space.

"I have an appointment."

She eyes him now, her eyebrows arching, annoyed and assessing in one throw. A bottle rises above the lip of benches where it has seemingly sat in her lap through this exchange. Square bottle, half empty, something dark. She slogs back a decent throw, wipes her mouth on the sleeve of a demure button-down, gray and professional.

"You're the salesman."

Her voice is sultry now, wet with drink. He nods. She speaks again.

"Someone should've called you."

He moves along the central aisle until he reaches her bench. Somewhere the sound of air conditioning stalls and a slow heat creeps in. He sits, not by her but at the bench's end, unhurried and unengaged, only pausing as he realizes his meeting is canceled and his purpose is unclear.

"Drink?"

He shakes his head without looking at her.

"Should I come back?" he asks.

She waves him off as she takes another pull.

"Don't bother. They'll phone in the order. No harm."

"My commission."

She waves this off as well, not bothering to clarify whether this wave means not to worry about the commission or not to expect it. Silence floods in for seconds. He waits until he can't and he fills that void with talk.

"It's ironic, though."

"What is?"

"The church. It's empty because everyone is at a funeral."

"What do you mean?"

"Don't people have funerals in churches?"

She shrugs.

"Some do."

She holds out the bottle. He turns. She leans to put it closer to where he sits. This time he takes it. He drinks, slow at first, then more and faster, feeling spiced fire burn its way down his gullet. He passes the bottle back. She speaks as she takes it.

"Do you like what you do?"

"Like what?"

"Like your job."

He moves closer, not to her but to the bottle. She passes it to him and he drinks. He wipes his mouth and speaks.

"It's a pointless existence. I drive around the country telling people to look at the website, order off the website. I'm living, breathing spam."

She laughs and snorts, an open guffaw absent of shame. He nods and takes a drink. They sit that way, passing drink from hand to hand, each facing front, two strangers separated by only a foot or two and nothing else in this world. Air conditioning kicks back in and the light finger of breeze caresses hot skin.

"Who died?"

"Does it matter?"

"Not to me," he says.

A violent awakening. His body lurches forward where it sits, yanking Charlie to consciousness. Eyes open in time, hands draped across legs propped in place, head hanging in the gulf between knees. Tie loose, turned and wrong. A line of saliva runs from lip to floor. He wipes his mouth and waits for the world to resolve itself.

A mechanical throb emanates from somewhere unseen. Air conditioner. The fall of night is felt in evidence though no window lets in the absence of sun. The heat has not abated but is instead hunkered, prone and waiting. Alcohol sweat drenches clothes. The brush of machine-cooled air across flesh is a welcome presence, but the taste of wood varnish is gone and the thin air smells of nothing.

He rises to his feet, only knowing he'll do so as the task is found completed. Slow turn, taking in the room. The change in light is a noticeable shift, darkness moving among the light. Nothing manages the clanging noise of being and the cacophonous background bleat that hides behind the everyday is now somehow absent. He is alone in this place.

He breathes in and out, allowing a moment to slip by. Hands are numb as they push open the door separating this consecrated realm from what lies beyond. Heat slicks skin, drops slipping down ribs and gathering on upper lip. He licks that salt taste and reels into the night in recommence of some task of which he holds no memory, unharried by hands of strangers that are not there.

5.

Check-in isn't for hours. The hotel lobby is deserted. He drinks gas station coffee from a styrofoam cup and waits for a bellhop or concierge to get tired of seeing him as they walk by and someone let him check in early. He wants to take meetings before the bigger vendors show up and soak all the business. He wants to sleep before the first night of the convention.

The chair is soft, expensive. Classy, or what he thinks of as classy. Subtle patterns in fabric. The sample case is nestled between scuffed shoes, loose socks. He's drunk and hung over. He's awake and asleep. Limbs hang loose in lap and that one hand clutches the warm cup of cheap brew with a genuine ferocity. A death grip. A sickened state has washed in and stayed. He sips the coffee.

Jaundiced tiling lines the ceiling, its surface decorated with patterns of a delicate intricacy, an inexplicable symmetry attained within that grand expanse. Eyes track the tangled designs as they work their way from the spot directly above to the far end of the lobby, the designs and their meaning becoming lost somewhere in the distance but still he looks to those lines, hoping with the vanity of a simple man that he might find his way.

"The smoking man."

Charlie's eyes pull with reluctance from the realm above to find a man paused midstep, arms flung from body, this suspension of stride abrupt. Goon in dented bowler. The goon smiles, looks around for chair, arms still hanging in interrupted imperative.

"Right? From the kids table."

Charlie points with coffee hand.

"You're following me."

Hands drop to sides, legs still installed in awkward walk stance. The goon's voice comes out devoid of emotion, a flat chorus of words barely interested in their own inquiry.

"Is there some reason I would follow you? Is there a reason anyone would?"

"I've seen you."

"You've seen me."

"What do you want?"

"Can't it all just be some coincidence?"

Charlie offers only a vacuous stare in return. The goon's shoulders sink on his frame, something unhinged, wires cut. One hand removes that outdated hat while the other rubs an unclean shock of hair, greased spikes lingering where they're left. He looks into the hat for an absent wisdom, finds nothing, puts that dented lump back on head.

"You're drunk," says the goon.

Charlie documents this stranger's egress with his own clouded gaze until focus dissolves and attention is once more taken with the cryptic meanderings overhead. He finishes his coffee in slow sips and when it's gone he wishes there were more.

———

The room looks expensive and he doesn't know where he is. He is awake for untold minutes before becoming resigned to this. The television is huge and there is a fish tank against one wall. Bizarre creatures move in aimless circuits forever between the limited walls of that water's intense blue. On TV a newsman prattles on about a doctor turned clown wanted for one scandalous thing or another. This is not the room Jess reserved for Charlie. Bigger, nicer. More time passes as details filter through. He changed the room, he remembers this. He remembers paying with the company card. He doesn't know why.

The bathroom is heaven bright. Every surface is a shined white reflecting and swelling the fierce pulse of harsh overhead bulbs. He runs water over his hands, lets it slip into the sink and down the drain, touches his face with wet hands, does this again. The water is cool, soft on skin. He leaves his hands there, feeling the caress of that flow for minutes. Soaps line the counter in elaborate wax wrappings, multicolored treats like high-born candies. He leans over, sniffs. Their scent is pleasant, something exotic. He doesn't unwrap them, doesn't want to upset that perfect array. He wipes his hands on his pants.

There is a clock lit up on the dresser but he doesn't look. It could be day or night. Moorings have come untethered. The sample case sits at the foot of the bed. Its clasp is fastened and contents safe. The necktie's knot has been unraveled. The tongue of cloth drapes from bed to floor. Charlie stands slackjawed and expectant, unsure of what it is he waits on. He reaches to his neck and unbuttons his collar. He doesn't lock the door behind him as he leaves.

Hall carpet swallows all sound. Footsteps make no noise at all, erasing the comings and goings of unseen traffic. No one leaves rooms, enters rooms, no light laughter coming from behind walls. The hotel is a house of ghosts, a place long ago left forlorn and empty. Charlie wanders in silence.

Turns and walking and there are no signs in this place. A man appears, an unmoving watcher in this void. Old, elderly a bent and wrinkled thing in undershirt behind glass. A brown cigarette hangs from the aged man's lip. Smoking enclosure, a balcony where a room should be. The man doesn't move, only stands in his windowed cage exhaling plumes of gray air. Beyond the man there is darkness. Night has come.

Elevators stand open as Charlie comes upon them, as if someone has just stepped out, but no one is around, no sounds of footsteps or room doors slamming shut. He steps in, presses a button. Wipes his face, presses the button again. Gravity shifts underfoot, a trusted companion acting out, proving unreliable. Stomach churns at the jolt of nature. Doors part. Ground floor.

Even here the sound is enormous, the static pattern of overlapping voices, innumerable exchanges intermixed, an amalgamation of talk. He moves down the corridor and through that wall of noise, pushing through its physical presence and to the door leading into the convention hall, one of them, lines of tables partitioning the room into its own loose maze navigated by faces eager with unashamed want. Smiling blond kids cut through the crowd handing out programs listing events and guest speakers. The singer from a band famed for updating traditional hymns with catchy pop riffs signs autographs at the head of a line stretching around her booth and away. Books are sold, apocalyptic tales with bright-lettered titles. The room is cooled by industrial venting high in the rafters. It breathes on Charlie as he stands in the way of that mouth, those open doors.

He doesn't go in.

The hotel bar is dim, its weak light thick in the air, a congealed glow drifting without purpose. He orders a drink but doesn't touch the glass as it's placed between splayed hands, only lets it sit sweating on the chipped wood bar. He pays with the company card. A pale man in a black coat sits drinking nearby. He does not look at Charlie. A phone buzzes in Charlie's pocket.

A woman sits down at the bar. She buys a drink, drinks it in gulps, eyes ringed in painted-on shade absorbed with the muted news show playing on a television screwed into the wall. On the screen is the same mad clown story as played in Charlie's room. The woman laughs at something, looks around to see if anyone notices. Those eyes find Charlie looking at her. She smiles, offers words both vague and kind, but she is not a woman he knows and this is not somewhere he wants to be. He does not tell her this, doesn't think it himself in something so lucid as words. Charlie drinks his drink.

The corridor hasn't changed, that wall of noise pushing against all who pass. Charlie doesn't look into the auditorium as he moves by. That noise follows around corners and down passages and doesn't relent in its pursuit. Elevator doors close it out but still it is felt if not heard, hands of noise grabbing hold and clutching tight. Charlie presses the button for what he thinks is his floor.

The walk to his room is a daze. Images float by in laissez-faire glimpses. Elevators opening, woman dropping purse in hall, old man smoking, smoking still or again, walking on until the door is there and he is inside. He doesn't hear the phone ringing in his pocket until he has it in hand, has brought it out. He stares without comprehension as a name comes across the readout and ringing goes on and then silence. He sits on the bed. The tie falls to the floor, where he reaches for it, drapes it around his neck, lies back on a pillow fluffed beyond reason. He looks at the name on the phone until the screen goes dark. Brings it back up and dials for voicemail. Missed calls spill out, Jess talking about the meetings he did not attend, asking questions he doesn't know the answers to, relaying information he doesn't care about. More calls, more Jess. Concerned, then angry, crying. He listens to every message and then he listens to each one again.

———

Saturday morning. He shaves in no rush. He splashes water on face and admires the way it beads and rolls off as it would from the surface of some nonporous facade, a plastic artifice he wears for a face. He pats dry with an unused towel.

His suit is cleaned and pressed, left on the bed by an unseen maid. He dresses and readies things, sets the sample case on the smoothed coverlet. The tie hangs untied from his neck. It stays that way as he shuts the door behind him.

The morning's first meeting isn't for twenty minutes. Coffee percolates among arrayed continental breakfast selections. He drinks two cups, then drinks another. He asks a woman setting out donuts to straighten his tie. She smiles. His tie isn't even tied. He tells her thanks when she's done, but she's already walked away. A man with eyes made large behind thick eyeglasses attempts and fails to engage in conversation about pastries and names, foreign words that mean nothing in this place.

"Wiener bread," he says. "Wiener brod."

Charlie drinks his coffee without acknowledging the man's expulsions.

First meeting is straightforward. Charlie talks books, buyer talks needs and wants. Prices aren't haggled, only spoken and understood. Charlie knowingly pronounces her name wrong. She corrects him with a smile. It's a dull name, generic syllables in prosaic amalgam. Her purchase tops out at a few grand.

It goes on this way, meeting after meeting for hours, some buyers picking up only a few dozen books or re-upping old contracts, others making deals for far more than they need. Charlie wades through the mess of it all glad-handing behind vapid smiles and affable nods. Conventions are all the same.

Evening comes on in a mad rush. Vendors gather in the hotel lounge drinking hard liquor and weak beer. Guests are off at a show, a concert played by some famous somebody no one's ever heard of. Merchants of religious trinkets and promoters of shows, publishers of pamphlets and all the rest, misfits populate the uninspired arrangement of tables, each man drinking and not discussing God. Stories are traded, tokens of ephemeral friendship. Men laugh at bad jokes and buy another round. Charlie sips at a glass of some oily libation paid for by a stranger, he knows not who. The case of sample books sits nestled under his chair. He listens, not hearing, to each pedestrian anecdote passed around like sage offerings, quietly drinking his way into his second drunk in as many days.

The smack of a palm on wood raises heads. A man at a distant table spreads out cards along his table where he's apparently just slapped them down. He shows around a mean grin, stopping to make sure each man before him has noticed its presence. The goon sits at that card-playing table, watching the glazed wet eyes of the grinning fool. Observers of this drama lose interest one by one, and the outcome of that game is uncertain.

Charlie takes a cigarette from a pack stowed away in some inner pocket, places the bent smoke in lips. He lights and inhales and ignores the looks from other tables. Someone mentions drinks, more drinks, and jabs a finger at member after member of these gathered conspirators to see who needs more. Charlie waves off the pointing man, offers to get the drinks himself. Men cheer as if a war has been won, and maybe it has. The sample case goes with him, is not left alone. He blows smoke as he crosses the room.

The bar is tended by a wholly new crew, none of the faces familiar from the night before. Charlie slaps the company card on the bar and orders a drink for himself. The pale man in the black coat perched on a stool to his left holds an unlit cigar. The pale man gestures with that fat brown roll at the cigarette hanging from Charlie's mouth.

"Seems you have a choice to make."

Charlie's head makes slow, half drunk rotation.

"What?"

"You keep drinking or you go on smoking that and they throw you out."

The drink arrives. Charlie holds onto the cool glass. He breathes smoke as he talks.

"You look like an undertaker."

The pale man looks him over.

"You look like a salesman."

"I am a salesman."

"How about that."

Charlie goes on waiting for the pale man to elaborate. The man returns only a stoic nothing. Charlie takes his glass and his cigarette and he walks away from the bar and the lounge, indifferent to watching eyes as he moves past the merchants left waiting for drinks that will never come.

Night air bathes skin with oppressive wet heat. The parking lot is full of cars but empty of people. Sounds of traffic echo through cityscape canyons. The glass Charlie holds sweats condensation that drips from fingers. He drinks and he smokes and when the one is gone he lights another. When the drink is gone he sets the glass on the hot macadam and wishes he'd brought along a second when he left the bar.

A thick man with no neck emerges from the hotel's lounge entrance. He drags the goon by a sulking shoulder. The two argue out of earshot, the goon gesticulating with wild abandon, the thick man unmoved by this display. The outcome of this encounter is decided long before the thick man turns away, the door closing behind him to shut that world away.

The goon sees Charlie watching him.

"Fuck 'em. Let's drink."

Charlie drops his cigarette.

"What'd you do?" he asks.

"They said I was cheating."

"They didn't care you were playing cards?"

The goon studies the words.

"Maybe that was it. Anyway," he looks over his shoulder. The door is still closed. "Fuck 'em."

His boots tromp away across the parking lot, thick thumps felt more than heard.

"I know a place," he says, not turning. "You play cards?"

Purposeful stride in and out of humbly lit worlds made by buzzing streetlamps. Charlie and the sample case are drawn in his wake.

———

The house is barely standing. Decrepit and leaning, a crippled being of warped, rotting boards. Around that feeble structure is an overgrown lot filled with a tangle of weeds parted only by the dual tracks of invading wheels. Buses and trucks in blunt pastels line the back end of the lot, a city block of transports parked and waiting. The face of a clown marks the side of a bus. Impassive eyes in a painted face. Charlie stops to look but the goon marches on through weeds, not stopping or giving up so much as a glance to the line of mismatched vehicles or the wild paints they wear.

"What is this place?"

The goon ignores Charlie, raps a knuckle on the door. Music trickles between boards, inarticulate humming and the thump of errant base. The door opens. The noise gains substance. Enthusiastic pop hit from a lost age. A diminutive woman smiles through the cracked door, nods up at the two men, opens the door wider. Charlie follows the goon through a twist of dim rooms, the goon navigating each turn like he's been here a hundred times. The music swallows footsteps and thoughts. Charlie is lost almost at once.

Nerves are shot by the time they come to their destination. The music encroaches on every thought, fighting to unhinge sanity entirely. Fading paint marks the door the goon presses his way through. A small room. Smoke drifts from lit cigarettes and open mouths. A room of bland faces, each indistinguishable from the next, but for the woman with the beard. She nods at the newcomers, they all do, and a card game stalled by this intrusion takes up its course anew. Cards laid down.

"Four."

A gruff voice loosing meaningless words, but the table's residents groan and the cards spell doom. The goon takes a seat at a chair left empty as if he's been expected.

"You coming?"

Someone pulls a chair from a closet full of them and a space is cleared for Charlie. The shuffling of cards sounds like childhood bike rides.

"Flat poker," says the shuffler with the gruff voice, some placid skull with an unremarkable mask of flesh to cover its banality. "Upright, respectable."

He deals and they play. Money is tossed with abandon into the pot, won and lost and on for hours. Charlie loses himself in the game, in the noise of conversations that mean nothing to him, talk of places and people he will never see, will never meet. A glass is set before him and when it is drained they fill another. Coins are bet along with cash and larger wagers, exotic coins from far off places and times, their worth only guessed at. He laughs at jokes he does not get and he is shocked when he reaches to make a bet after some untold hours and finds his pockets empty of cash.

"You got a card?"

Charlie's gaze falls to the table and the cards and cash and coins in front of each player. It falls further still, to the floor and to his feet. He nods.

"Hit an ATM. Chair's yours now. It'll be here when you get back."

The bearded lady waves as he leaves.

The sky is a forlorn blue wash above an empty world. The chronic noise of traffic comes from a distant place, but nothing stirs here in these streets and the only movement is a hot breeze and the blink of signs peddling irrelevant wares. Morning has come.

He walks the few blocks it takes to find a lit gas station. Bell chimes his arrival. Inside is a buzzing light and row after row of identical items. The card is fed into the ATM mouth and cash is given in thanks. He grabs a water and moves to the counter.

"That it?"

The cashier is uninterested in this presence, his question a perfunctory cough of syllables. Charlie points past the man.

"And a bottle of that."

He doesn't know what he points at, and it doesn't matter.

"It's not even seven, man."

Charlie's face is an empty thing.

"Can't sell alcohol this early."

He pays for the water with the company card.

The walk back takes his lonely footsteps past a church whose parking lot has begun to accumulate stern children with tired eyes and perfumed parents chatting as they walk toward open doors. Some may be faces from the bar or the convention hall. Charlie glances their way, but if he's seen them before this moment he does not know.

The game still goes on as he returns to the bent house and its dark inner room. A final hand of some arcane contest plays out, each player passing a card from his or her own hand to the person seated to the left. Charlie watches but doesn't follow. The goon nods as he lays down his cards. The losers moan. Charlie sits in the still empty chair.

Whatever the name of the game just ended, no word of it is spoken as a standard hand of poker is once more dealt. After that is another, and more from there. Hours go by and money changes hands. A rhythm develops, drinks poured and stories told and the bearded lady watches Charlie as he plays each hand. He sees her watching and she smiles. When the money is gone and there's nothing left to stay in the game Charlie doesn't think twice about betting the company car.

The carnies offer him a ride to his next stop when it's over.

The road between towns is dark when they leave the leaning, warped house. The line of trucks cut through the miles with professional determination. Charlie sleeps the whole way. The phone is dead and the charger is in the sample case but he does not charge it, does not want to know about the appointments he's missed, does not want to think about the convention. The calls can wait. It is night again and Sunday has been lost.

The sun isn't up when he's dropped off. The dull blue creeping into the sky says morning is on the way. A payphone outside a fast food outlet hangs from its cradle like a beacon of a lost age. Charlie doesn't bother digging through pockets for quarters, he's lost them all and he knows this. A woman gives him change as she leaves the eatery.

He dials with numb fingers. He knows she's going to cry when she answers, she's going to shout and she does. She doesn't understand and he doesn't know how to explain. He apologizes because he doesn't know what else to do. She cries again. He nods but she doesn't see. The sun is rising as he tells Jess the company car's been stolen.

6.

The rental is filled with the cloying sweet stink of new car. Charlie looks in the glove box and in pockets behind seats but no air freshener is found. Lines in the floor and seats define where someone has recently vacuumed. The odometer reads fifty thousand miles.

He checks his face in the mirror. Pools of vibrant purple bruise show under eyes sunken deep into a skull. Stubble marks cheeks and jaw. A nap and a shower have not set things to rights. He unplugs his phone from the charger and stares at the itinerary without recognition for what may be minutes. He puts it away when he's had enough.

The meeting isn't for forty minutes. Not the standard appointment, no office or church building. The rental sits parked outside a gray box of a building. City gymnasium. A song plays on the radio as the sky turns the hazy red of imagination. When he's tired of waiting he goes inside. The meeting isn't for twenty minutes.

They don't hear him come in, or if they do they don't turn. They sit in a circle, lonely faces filling plastic seats. They talk amongst themselves. Charlie stays at the edges, doesn't interrupt. Snacks wait on a table against one wall. Pastries and things. A grease-stained box once held donuts. Coffee sits burning away in an ancient coffeemaker. He pours a cup and drinks as he waits listening.

"We used to run across the street. It was a game, you know? Wait till a car comes and then go. The closer the car, the better you did. We didn't keep score, we just, it just made sense."

A pause opens in the story of the thin stranger it belongs to. Seconds stretch in that silent gulf. A slow horror dawns inch by haunted inch on a face that pales as time wears on. Eyes glaze as the man looks into some distant locale existing now only for him.

"We were kids. We couldn't die."

A face comes up from among the gathered circle, a priest's collar ringing his neck. The priest finds Charlie at the room's edge.

"We'll have to stop there for the evening."

The thin man looks to the priest with hollow eyes, some part of his story swallowed untold. The priest shakes the hands of the gathered as they stand and depart through any of several gymnasium doors. The thin man whispers with the priest as they shake, the priest putting a hand on shoulder, the thin man nodding as the priest whispers back. Solemn words. Charlie looks away from their talk and soon the thin man is gone.

"You have my books?"

The priest does not shake Charlie's hand.

"I'm just here for the order."

A wrinkled brow and pursed lips twist the priest's face.

"That's right," he says.

Charlie points at the circle of empty chairs.

"What were they talking about?"

"This is a private group."

"I was only asking."

"Asking what that man was talking about."

"Yes."

The priest examines Charlie's face and words with a wary interest.

"You're welcome to join. Something you want to talk about?"

Charlie looks away, his eyes unfocused.

"What is it you want to talk about?"

Charlie shrugs. The priest's voice comes out in a soothing lilt.

"Do you dream?"

"That's a stupid question."

"Is it stupid because you do or because you don't?"

"I dream. Everybody does."

"What do you dream?"

"Puzzles and things. Normal things."

"What are normal things?"

"I dream about monsters and memories, pets I had as a kid, whatever. I dream I'm back in school and I can't find my way home."

The priest smiles.

"You should join our group."

Charlie holds up his sample case.

"Here for business."

The priest nods.

"I don't need much."

"What do you need?"

"A dozen," says the priest, eyes rolling at the thought. "Maybe less. Half a dozen."

"You don't need me for that. A half dozen." "Well?"

Charlie's eyes search the room for a computer, something with internet. There is nothing. His website spiel won't work here.

"Fuck it."

"What?" says the priest. The word is casual, amused.

Charlie opens the sample case, takes out a stack of books with each hand. He holds them out before him like some bizarre offering, three bound volumes in each hand.

"What?" repeats the priest, the casual tone hardened, cautious.

"Take them."

The priest doesn't touch them, instead pointing to the table with its burned coffee and stale crumbs. Charlie sets the books among the refuse.

"I can write you a check, whatever you want," says the priest.

Charlie looks into the priest's eyes. He recognizes nothing he finds there.

"I don't want anything."

———

He parks beside the old black hardtop and works his way through a slow cigarette, lighting and holding and not thinking or even smoking but just waiting unfeeling for minutes. When he goes inside he leaves the phone in the car.

The room is an unlit fog, bare bulbs here and there giving form to portions of world among the otherwise darkened gloom. Shapes shift in that darkness, whispering voices without mouths that move about more felt than seen in the periphery. Charlie sees the face of a familiar stranger at the bar.

"Hello, salesman."

The pale man turns his oval face on Charlie's approach. Slight nod at an empty stool and nothing more. Charlie orders a drink. He swallows it down in repetitive, determined pulls from the glass. When it's gone he orders another.

"What do you sell, salesman?"

The book Charlie pulls from the mouth of the sample case is a muted red number, its title wrought in gold.

"Gods," says Charlie.

The pale man's eyes move from the book to Charlie, narrowing, studying.

"A religious man."

"Not particularly."

Charlie says it without thought, a matter-of-fact string of words. He takes a drink.

"A charlatan, then."

"And what do you do?"

"I drive," says the pale man.

"Drive what?"

"A car, charlatan."

Charlie orders another drink. It comes and he drinks to numbing excess, unaware of what he already does not feel.

He offers bits of conversation, but the pale man drinks his drink in a spreading pool of silence as inane chatter begins to leak from Charlie's drunken form.

"I drive, too. Everywhere. I used to walk. When I lived in one place. In the city? Now I have a place in some suburb I never see. I drive everywhere now. For work, you know."

The room noise swells around him, a hum of life rising with each sip he takes. His own voice grows to meet that hum, to stand above it and be heard even though he has nothing to say.

"I feel like I could start walking in any direction forever and I'd never come to anything new."

The pale man drinks and says nothing. When Charlie is done with his drink he leaves the book behind as he goes.

A room is rented somewhere in his name, a spot picked out just for Charlie, but he makes it only as far as the car before the weight of the world pulls him under. He cracks the window and curls in the seat and only seconds pass before he is gone.

———

He makes the call to the office before he is awake. A hand pushes knuckle-first into blurred eyes, attempting and failing to wipe sleep away. The voice that answers is unfamiliar and terse. He wants to ask about Jess but he doesn't.

The day's morning appointments are rote events, smiles and handshakes and exchanges and done, quid pro quo at its most banal. He tells jokes that mean nothing and strangers laugh as they fork over cash to the indefinable essence represented so feebly by the outdated website. The day proceeds.

Sun falls. The day's last meeting is on the outskirts of town, a last piece of civilization skirting the edge of nothing. Lines of bunched trees close off the property from view along the street and create a barrier marking this land as the buffer between a housing subdivision to one side and an emptiness to the other. The untrimmed grasses that shroud this place are a color all their own, the green of cartoons and childhood imagination, a vibrant thing in contrast to the subdued fields of waving stalks beyond the growth of trees.

Charlie maneuvers the rental along a driveway weaving its indirect course through the trees and onward into a cleared plot at whose heart sits a sprawling, monstrous house. The mansion is a dilapidated horror, a former hotspot for passing hopelessness in a decade long gone. The place is famous for having belonged to a celebrity no one remembers. It had a name once, this estate, a tacky moniker dubbed by some new-money oaf. A circular drive whose face was once paved is now broken and jagged, long cracks running along its uneven surface giving way to the sprouting growth that will someday reclaim this place. Charlie parks in the grass.

No lights show in windows whose glass has long since been smashed in. Charlie waits and watches the house a moment, listening to the life to one side, televisions on in a thousand homes, the buzzing of streetlamps, the passage of cars and time, and to the other side only a soft wind washing with tender caress across the tops of uncut fields.

He pulls out his phone.

Jess's home isn't the first number he dials, but it is the first call made that he sticks with until voicemail picks up. A months-old recording of her voice delivers the custom spiel. He waits for the beep before he can let himself hang up. He leaves no message. He doesn't call a second time.

The steps are bent at ends, their nails loose in sockets like the teeth of an addict, rickety and treacherous. The groan of old wood cuts through the noises of those other worlds as Charlie mounts each step.

The front door is unlocked. He enters without knocking. A hallway leads the way between walls, its faded carpet worn down from feet and dust and years. Stairs lead off and up in a nook to the left that he ignores completely. Lighter spots along walls show where pictures or paintings once hung. A soft tapping emanates from a place deep within the mansion's unlit middle.

Hall leads to rooms and rooms give way to more of the same as the delicate drumbeat of a mechanical chatter grows closer. Charlie finds the dining hall without purpose, only another space opening before him among the many. He is surprised to find a man hunched at the end of a long table marching through determined keystrokes in the dark without looking up. The man acknowledges Charlie's arrival with a nod.

"Sit, if you like."

The room is crumbling but swept, a thing in transition. Wallpaper hangs in places, its once crisp lines and patterns faded or gone altogether while letters mark the surface of one wall in sprawling, manic graffiti. *SAVE YOURSELF*. A pristine couch sits indifferent to the despair by which it is surrounded. Clean floral-patterned cushions remind the room of better times. Charlie sits. Words form on lips and a finger points at the sample case sitting at his feet, but he's cut off when the typing man speaks first.

"Don't worry about the selling spiel. Order's already placed."

Charlie should ask questions. He should ask which editions were ordered and what styles, questions about delivery method or why this place needed to be on the list of stops if the order didn't need Charlie in order to be placed, but instead he cuts right to it.

"How many?"

The man doesn't stop typing.

"Ten thousand copies."

The soft slap of finger on keys moves at an unsteady pace, its current rising and falling with the motion of whatever unseen force exists on the other side of that screen. The typing man throws out a casual addition to his statement, never looking up.

"You'll get your piece."

Charlie leans back, slowly sinking into the cushions. A light perfume blooms, the sweet smell of someone sitting in this place just before. He breathes in their scent as his head reels.

"You look tired," says the typing man, not looking.

"Ten thousand is a lot."

"Ten thousand is just the right number," says the typing man.

"What will you do with ten thousand books?"

The typing man considers the question, or he pretends to as he types.

"There is a hole in men. They fill it with drugs or with work or with the lie that it isn't there, that there's no hole at all, but it is there, and I mean to address that. Civilizations have been built on a common idea, and no idea unites disparate peoples like hope. Hope is purpose. Hope is something beyond the maintenance of everyday life. Do you believe that?"

Charlie answers with absolute sincerity.

"I don't know."

Moments pass in which the only sound is the light keystroke rhythm. The typing man breaks the quiet.

"Do you have that?"

"What?"

"Hope."

Charlie shrugs. He looks at the man at the table, fingers tapping in the dark.

"Do you believe any of it?" asks Charlie

"Any of what?"

"What you just said. The whole thing."

"Would you feel better if I said yes?"

Charlie leans over. His head rests on the cushioned couch arm, a plush thing that conforms to this pressure. The scent is stronger here, a fading memory of something pleasing.

"You look tired," the typing man says again.

Charlie's phone begins to buzz in his pocket. He pulls it out and the buzzing becomes a ringing. The name displayed there catches breath and squeezes gut. Heart beats too fast and blood inundates head. He stares at the display and hopes a decision will come.

"You gonna get that?"

Charlie goes on staring until the ringing falls away.

"No," he says.

He doesn't know this place. Sunlight streams in through a doorway leading off and away, and only as he supports himself with one hand on the floor and strains to look around the corner and into the next room does he see that light's source is a hole where once a window had been. The frame remains, but the glass is broken out and the boards are warped from years of disregard. It is a rich light, that sun, the storybook feel of fresh light felt as much as seen.

It comes back to him a piece at a time; the crumbling mansion, the typing man, the world. Charlie looks around but the typing man is gone and he is alone in this place. He straightens his tie but it looks wrong. He checks his phone. He's late for the morning's meeting. There are no missed calls.

He drives too fast and runs as many lights as possible. The rental smells wrong, a half-burnt musk filtering in through the AC. He closes the vents and turns up the radio. He arrives and parks and runs through halls with the sample case dragging down one side of his shambling, determined form. He looks at the bathroom door as he passes, wonders for only a moment if he should go in, brush teeth, splash water on a face still creased from sleep.

The meeting plays out as every meeting does. His lateness goes wholly unnoticed.

He rushes through the particulars, the scant few half-necessary moments his day requires, shakes a hand belonging to someone he won't remember in five minutes, and escapes with a purpose back into the day. The sun is brighter now as he steps beneath its reach, a harsh white glare that went overlooked in the rush that brought him here. He wishes for sunglasses or a hat. He steps under an awning with others who share his motive for undertaking the pilgrimage to this sidewalk haven. He lights a cigarette.

"Can I get one of those?"

A little man in a long coat asks the question with a timid hope. Charlie shakes one from the pack, hands it over without word. The little man nods.

"Nobody smokes anymore," says the little man by way of meager conversation. "You work here?"

Charlie shakes his head.

"I'm a bible salesman."

Smoke escapes the little man's mouth as he laughs.

"Nobody does that anymore, either."

———

The drive between cities is hours long, that unconquered span between places a vast and wild thing. Day wears on. One song follows another as the noise that streams from the radio becomes an indecipherable blend of catchy pop noise. He turns up the volume and loses himself in the hours.

Day becomes night. No one passes and no one is met and Charlie is alone in this place between places. Towns come and go, lonely places marked only by old signs and turnoffs leading toward things that might be. A world slips by, immense expanses seen but not felt by transients who move between these open wilds on their way to some civilized locale. Those strangers are not here now but signs remain long after they've passed; holes in signs where someone has squarely put bullets, a can resting in dust at the shoulder. Somewhere off in a field of tall grass is a car overturned and rusted, the forgotten mark of some long-ago calamity.

An undramatic light pops on among the instruments and gauges of the dash display. The symbol there means something to someone who has read the car's manual, but Charlie only gapes at this inexplicable intrusion. His eyes lose the road but there is nothing there to see. The warning light remains and he goes on staring, wondering at its meaning.

7.

He lost the company car a thousand miles ago. The rental has been dead for hours, broken and spent in a ditch outside a town no one's ever heard of. He can't hear his shoes as they slap endlessly on the pavement but he knows he is still moving. The moon isn't full but it's close enough to call it that. The air has a thick feel to it. It isn't raining but it smells like it's about to or maybe just has. He carries only one bag. His left side hangs lower than the right with the weight of it. The sound of tires on gravel and the warning groan of an engine aching to roar is noticeable but he pretends it isn't.

"Ride somewhere?"

He doesn't look over and if he can't see the pale man he isn't there. The engine laughs gasoline chortles but doesn't rev and the black beast crawls along beside Charlie, waiting.

"I think I'll walk for awhile."

The pale man shifts his body inside the car. His attention slips. Charlie looks with only the barest edge of notice as the pale man spins the dial on the radio as far as it will go, static all the way. It's the old kind, a small tack and a bunch of numbers backlit by a single orange bulb. Everything about the car is like that. Old. One of those long black hardtops, '50s maybe, the way they used to be when gasoline was nothing and the rage in that engine was everything. Whitewalls spin achingly slow as the beast paces along.

"A long way to any place you want to find yourself. Might be nobody else will come along tonight."

He turns a long, oval face up to that great moon touching every corner of the night sky. He touches his strange, misshapen face with long fingers.

"Might be someone not so friendly will come along."

The one bag grows heavier in Charlie's left hand and his arm throbs with the weight of it. Muscles jump underneath the skin and fingers clamp desperately onto the handle. Shoes are worn through on the bottoms and the gravel of pavement stings with every step. Breath comes in deep, slow dips that he takes and holds, takes and holds. He stares straight ahead as he walks.

"I'll find my way."

The pale man opens a sleek silver lighter with Lenin's face on the side and some writing too blurred to see and he puts flame to a fat cigar the color of coffee. The smell fills the night with a sweet, strong odor. Charlie breathes and takes a step, breathes and steps.

"What's your name?" says the pale man with a voice that's a low rumble, words like the belly laugh of a giant. Charlie's arm twinges. He wants to switch the bag to his right hand but not in front of this apparition.

"What's yours?"

No look is needed to see the mouth open and that smoke roll out through that smile. It is pleased.

"Be seeing you up the road, charlatan."

The last few words are almost lost as that great black beast ushers forth a roar of hate and purpose and screams into the night on four whitewalls unblemished by time or wear. His taillights are miles away when the night finally takes them once more in its dark hand. Only then does Charlie switch the bag from left hand to right and stop to breathe and rest.

He rests only a moment. He still has so far to go.

———

A dusty roadside bump of a town. A gas station along a dead stretch of highway around which trails lead off into hardpan hills to suggest life further attached to this far-flung outpost.

Charlie dusts himself off before going inside.

He watches the thin man's eyes that watch him back as Charlie ambles down one aisle and then another tipping packets of crackers into his open bag. He takes two bottles of water and sets the bag on the floor. A bell tolls somewhere behind the counter. The thin man watches Charlie's hand digging deep into one pocket and then another. He grumbles and keeps pretending to look through pockets he's already pretended to search. A door opens to the outside world. The scent of gas and asphalt. Cheap lotion on top. Charlie grumbles again, mostly noises, a few words. *I can't, Where is,* etc.

The man who comes to stand at Charlie's side is his height but older, old, the lines of his face etched and lived in. He stands straight, a posture of confidence. His hair is a shock of white and he smiles at everything. His teeth are square and long, too big for his mouth, blank domino tiles.

"Pack of whatever's on tap."

He points at a brand of cigarette no one's ever heard of. If there were a line at the counter he wouldn't notice. Charlie stops digging in pockets. The man exhales something like mouthwash and coffee and sets a hundred on the counter.

"For the gas. And."

He points at the off-brand cigarettes. The hand moves to encompass Charlie's items.

"His too."

The thin man looks at Charlie and at the man. He looks back at Charlie. He looks at Charlie for a long time. He takes the hundred and doesn't give the man any change. He doesn't say a single word throughout the exchange.

The man is in his car with the engine on. Silver late-model something. Charlie taps on the window.

"You need a ride."

Statement, not a question. Charlie nods.

"Where you going?"

Charlie points with chin, a minute gesture that means little.

"Up the road."

"I can take you part of the way. That all you got?"

The man looks at the bag pulling down Charlie at the shoulder. Charlie gets in without answering. The car is pulling into the road before the door is closed.

There is no talk for miles and Charlie messes with the radio without asking. Some people slap hands or scream for this but the man hums quietly to himself and says nothing. He grips the wheel with both hands and fingers make subtle flexes like he's pumping a hand accelerator.

"What brings you out here?"

Charlie doesn't know how to answer or maybe he hadn't considered the thought before now himself. He shrugs and the man takes that to mean whatever he wants.

"Your whole life in that bag?"

"Just some things. Essentials. My work."

"What do you do?"

"Nothing."

A phone rings in Charlie's bag but he ignores it and eventually it grows quiet once more.

The man looks at himself in the mirror from time to time. His grin falters but never leaves entirely. Those wide square teeth push out lips in loose Neanderthal chic. He hums. There is nothing on the radio.

"I see you looking."

Charlie isn't looking but he looks now.

"It's okay to ask," says the man.

"Where did you get them?"

The man throws back his head like he's going to laugh but he doesn't laugh and only goes on smiling. He speaks through the smile. Charlie cringes and doesn't know why.

"Somebody once told me if you see a traffic cop in your mirror in Mexico you just keep on driving. They just told me a few years too late."

He takes one hand from the wheel and unscrews the top from one of Charlie's bottles of water.

"I'll pay you back," he says as he takes a drink. He sets the bottle between his legs. He doesn't put the top back on.

"I was on my way back to the States when these lights come up on me, and me being a kid from the suburbs, back then I didn't know any better. I pull over and wait with my papers out. This old boy walks up, he doesn't ask to see my papers. He takes one look at me and has his measure. He has me get out of the car and he's looking in my back seat for something, he doesn't say what. He comes back and looks me over again and says I'm going to jail. I don't want to go to jail. Well he wants my cash. I'm broke and in Mexico just trying to get home and BAM a fist cracks my mouth wide the fuck open. I spit half my teeth onto the ground before I even know I've been hit. He rips my wallet and pocket out both and says something I don't understand and I'm lucky to be alive."

Charlie doesn't know what to say. Another person would say something nice. Polite, concerned.

"They did a good job fixing them," says Charlie.

"They wanted to fix em up just like they were, brand new. I told that doctor hell no! I'm from Texas. Everything's bigger in Texas, that's what they say, right?"

He looks at Charlie and not the road.

"Right?"

He looks at Charlie and not the road, those big square pearlies asking and judging.

"Right?"

Only Charlie and not the road.

"Yes."

"You're damn right it is! I told that bastard, make them sons of bitches fierce! I want a smile proud and blank, like a fucking unspent canvas, unsullied next time I run into that traffic cop done me that way."

Charlie's mouth is dry and sour and full of words and moving.

"That kind of thing probably happens to a lot of people. You were a kid. You think if you ever found this guy he'd really remember you?"

"Oh, I think he remembered me after awhile," says the man as he shows that flat domino grin.

———

He must have slept. It's morning and no time has passed. It could be any day. He gets out of the car and watches the man smile at the road. Black lines of rubber stretch into the distance after the man is gone but they are not from him. They go on for miles.

Charlie checks the time on his phone and looks at the sky. He runs his finger along the phone's screen and the itinerary it holds. He looks at the building at his back and looks back at the phone. A list of chores from a past life. He puts the phone away and pushes open a thick wooden door.

The room smells like an office building. A happy man tells Charlie he's expected as hands shake without affection. A young woman straightens a candelabra and doesn't look at Charlie. He walks between pews and follows the happy man through a doorway. An office, homey, all its edges soft. A laptop sits on a desk, the only thing at all businesslike. The screensaver is Beziers. He turns off a television. Morning news, an anchor like every other anchor. Turmoil left in the wake of a mad clown's rampage. The sound was mute before he turned the TV off but there is a squawk from speakers as the screen goes black. Charlie doesn't sit until the happy man sits first.

"I was beginning to think you weren't going to make it."

Charlie smiles without commitment.

"Let's see what you have for me."

Charlie opens the bag and takes out a single copy of the book. The pages are bound in an inviting soft blue leather cover. Calming to look upon. The happy man takes the book, holds it in a gentle grasp, like something that could get away from him at any moment.

"This is our top model. I won't say who told me but just between us girls, I hear the Vatican was jealous when they heard what we were putting out this year."

The happy man laughs and Charlie points to the laptop in *May I?* gesture. The man turns the computer halfway around. Charlie types at an awkward angle and resents the happy man.

The company website is boring and outdated. Samples come up. Charlie smiles like an idiot.

"Pick a color, any color. I like the blue."

The website shows a picture of the same sample held by the happy man. In the picture Charlie is holding the book. The site hasn't been updated in some time.

"Is there a minimum order?"

The question is common.

"We're used to dealing with congregations of at least a few hundred units but we do handle orders from the big chain churches. Larger orders are fine."

The happy man hides the envy that crosses his face, but it is there. Charlie takes a form from his bag and pretends to write down information as the man spouts it out. Numbers, addresses, paperwork standards. Charlie smiles and nods a lot. He shakes an offered hand and thanks the man and turns to leave but turns back.

"I can't do this."

Eyebrows dive into the middle of the happy man's face but he says nothing. Charlie sits in the silence for a beat. And then he's on.

"This isn't right. I look around at your place here, at your setup, and I can't do this. The publisher's been overcharging. These prices, they're marked up twenty percent from last year."

The happy man's face contorts. He wants to say something but he waits.

"Look, here's what I'm gonna do. I can order this under my employee code and get you the same order for half the cost."

Eyebrows slowly fall back into place. Posture softens by slow degrees.

"You can do that?"

Charlie has him.

"I like it here. I like this place. I can't keep doing this. I think this is my last call. I want it to be just right and I'm out. Do you, I mean, do you know where I'm coming from?"

The happy man stands and looks Charlie in the face. He puts a hand on Charlie's arm.

"I think I do."

Charlie digs in his bag for the phone. Missed calls. The battery is low.

"Let me call this in and we'll get your order filled right now."

"You won't get in trouble?"

Charlie sticks out his bottom lip like a sad three-year-old and his face scrunches as he shakes his head no. He pretends to dial and reads for the no one on the other end things he didn't write down from the blank form. He puts a hand over the phone and whispers.

"On hold."

The happy man nods with empathy.

"Okay, yes, yes thank you."

He hands up the phone and smiles.

"Okay, we're all done here. You can just make that check out to me and I'll get out of your hair."

8.

The teller is chewing gum that looks like plastic. It doesn't smell like mint and Charlie instantly mistrusts her. She asks for I.D. when he hands her the check. She asks if he has an account. She asks other questions and she chats about her kids and the weather and Charlie touches her hand when she hands him the envelope. Her neck and cheeks turn a nice shade of red.

The highway has a line of gas stations and fast food joints with names known better than those of presidents. Charlie walks from one to the next and in and out of truck stops looking at the clientele. Men who smell like gasoline.

Men who wear button-up shirts with lesser-known names on the tags. Men who don't fall into any category and could be anybody at all. Charlie looks them over and goes on to the next stop.

A woman with a pen in one hand and a bottle of ketchup in the other watches him come through the door and walk straight to her. An electronic chime of a bell rings above the door but its ring comes late. Her apron is clean but smells wonderful, like meat and God. Charlie asks her for a sheet of paper and she blinks only one eye.

The bathroom is around a corner and down a hallway. He scribbles TOILET BROKEN in big block letters on the sheet of paper and sticks it to the door. It stays without any tape. He locks the bathroom door when it closes behind him. He doesn't turn out the light as he curls up in a corner and in minutes he is lost in a deep sleep.

———

Ham-fisted beating brings back the world. Charlie opens eyes and the noise doesn't stop. He turns on the faucet as far as it will go but he still hears the fist on the door.

"I'm in here," he says in a weak voice. The water and the pounding drown the words completely.

He brushes teeth and touches a wet hand to a cold face. He blinks and picks up his bag and opens the door and a tiny frog of a man who says his name is Edgar after he is asked several times looks at Charlie strangely and goes into the bathroom as Charlie moves past. The man locks the door. Charlie leaves the sign where it is.

The woman with the ketchup no longer holds the pen or the ketchup. She holds nothing. She leans over the counter and watches the traffic going by outside. She thinks about places she'd rather be and she smiles when Charlie asks for something to eat.

"What would you like, hon?"

She says hon. Nobody has used that word in decades.

"I don't know."

And he doesn't. The question is too open and inviting. Too ambiguous and assured that maybe she will have or could find what he would like. She is too optimistic and she uses words like hon.

"Can I get a cup of coffee?"

He doesn't want coffee. He's seen so many movies that play out just like this, their plots leading along to nowhere. Clichés fill his mouth. He says as little as possible.

"What kind?"

What kind of what? What brand of coffee? What flavor? Do they have more than one flavor in no-name truck stop diners? This never happens in movies.

"Black."

This must be the right answer because the ketchup woman sets a blue mug of steaming liquid in front of Charlie almost instantly before wandering away. He can only gaze at it with longing, years of futile efforts having beaten in the knowledge that hot things burn. Mouth waters but he resists. He sits. He waits.

"You gonna drink that?"

Her dark hair is tied back and there's some kind of smudge on her brow, like she's just wiped her forehead after changing a tire and maybe beating a biker to death. She's tiny in the way adults sometimes are, average height and build but still somehow giving the impression that maybe she can fit in a pocket. She's familiar but Charlie has no idea why. She takes the next seat without a hint of self-consciousness. She doesn't bother asking if the seat is taken and he's glad she decided to sit.

"I just wanted to buy it and set it free."

She doesn't know if this is a joke and neither does he. Her fingers tap lightly on the countertop for a moment. He doesn't do anything as cliché or polite as offer a hand to shake. He pushes his cup of steaming black coffee over to her and asks the ketchup woman for another.

"Anything else?"

Meals skipped, each one ignored or forgotten now squeeze at his middle, make themselves known. He doesn't know what he wants, but he knows he wants something.

"Do you have grilled cheese?"

The waitress looks at him like it is absurd to ask whether or not they have grilled cheese in a nameless, faceless diner outfitted like the set for every nameless, faceless diner in every movie where a bland face in a colorless background orders a grilled cheese.

"And hash browns."

He can't think of anything else cliché to order so he stops talking. The ketchup woman's nametag doesn't say Flo, but he thinks of her as Flo anyway. She doesn't feel the need to write down his order. This is the order every patron of this establishment has ordered for decades.

"You're going to eat food here?"

The familiar face turns colorless eyes to Charlie, waiting. She chugs boiling coffee while looking on with horrified eyes.

"Other people are eating it."

She doesn't say anything, just looks at Charlie with a crooked face, eyebrows arched and ready to strike. They don't move when a charred square of wonder is placed on the counter on a featureless white plate, a small fort built from hash browns guarding the plate's flank. A crevice runs the length of the square where some heathen has cut it in half. The burnt shell on top contains hidden patterns. Charlie stares.

A throat clears, not his, he doesn't know whose. He's been looking at the sandwich sitting in front of him for a full minute. His lips are moving but he doesn't know what he's been saying.

"You can have it."

She smiles and still she looks at Charlie but he's looking at the food and seeing dead worlds and lives he hasn't lived in ages.

"You've earned it," is all she says. Flo walks by. The familiar face holds out a hand, points at the empty coffee cup, makes a circular motion. Keep 'em comin'. And they do.

Her eyes follow the sandwich as it moves to his mouth. She doesn't blink, doesn't look away as he takes each bite. She doesn't laugh or talk but only watches as the sandwich is wholly devoured. The plate is attacked with a feverish zeal, a hunger unexpected now coming to bear.

She watches as he eats every bite on the plate, and he does, he does eat every bite of hash brown, no morsel escaping his gaping maw. He looks at the plate and considers ordering more but his distended belly churns beneath and he lets it. He wants a glass of water but he doesn't wave someone down or ask random passersby for one.

The familiar face takes all this in and says nothing or at least very little, always a knowing, almost maternal look on her face that means nothing to him.

"Who are you," he says after awhile.

"What difference does it make? Who are you?"

"Nobody."

She stares like she may hit him. She smiles but that look is there, matronly and hostile all at once. There is a wrinkle in her nose that goes with the smile and Charlie knows he will see it every time he closes his eyes. He thinks about closing them.

She finishes his cup of coffee for him.

"I know who you are."

A pop and a stranger's yip of a scream and something like fire in the kitchen cuts through the moment and Charlie blinks once or twice as she walks out the door, the electronic chime of a bell the only thing he has to remember her by.

And that one beautiful wrinkle.

"Wait," he says, and catches the door before it can close.

———

Her place is a suite in a decent chain hotel. She walks in and leaves him to follow or not. She goes into the bathroom, a shadow going about some task among the light spilling through the open door. That shade meanders. Charlie looks away.

There was no talk on the drive over. She listened to the radio, or she turned it up and pretended to. Charlie kept his bag between his feet and watched this strange city play out before him. All the signs were the same, ominous portents broadcasting the notion that whatever he's running from has already spread here before his arrival.

The room is cooled by a swirl of breeze that circulates without end, stirring the thick sweet scent of unseen potpourri. The television is alive with scrolling text and a man in a suit delivering news about something from somewhere. A blur of information. Charlie doesn't notice her return until he feels the weight on the bed beside him. A bottle falls against his thigh. Amber liquid rolls and swirls inside. His phone rings once. He turns it off.

It's like this for days.

They fuck or they watch TV or they drink. She tells him she's in town on business and if it's a lie he accepts it as gospel anyway. She gives him a name that is not hers. He lets her be whoever she wants and she doesn't ask the wrong questions. They each understand how little they need to understand, and it works for a time.

She sweats whiskey in whatever unimaginable place she spends her days. Her attire is business casual, smart enough and sharp enough to suggest the professionalism of a cutthroat, just one unbuttoning away from a karaoke evening.

He spends the days alone. Game shows he hasn't seen in years are watched with a contained hostility. Court shows follow game shows, sad people fighting over a pittance. Televised bitterness. He orders room service and drinks until he vomits with a violence he is unprepared for. He sleeps and it all happens the same every day.

"Do you like what you do?"

Her voice is thick with drink. Not a slurring but a sensual wetness, a husk that pleads. She looks at him now, the question she has asked hanging between them, a line crossed or almost crossed.

"You don't know what I do," he says.

She takes a drink from the bottle. A pink tongue licks wet lips, the bitter dregs left there by the bottle's passing.

"What do you do?"

He takes the bottle from her. She gives it up and he drinks, wipes his mouth on his sleeve. He is looking at his legs stretched out before him on the bed when he answers, one sock pushed down and bundled around a pale ankle dotted with fine, tiny hairs.

"Do you go to church?"

She shrugs.

"Everybody goes to church," she says.

He looks at her.

"What does that mean?"

She takes the bottle back but doesn't drink.

"Everybody believes in something, even if that something is just that life should be lived for the sake of living. Even if that something is that life doesn't matter, it's still a belief. You can believe whatever, and you can do it wherever. So. I don't know."

He reaches for the bottle and she pulls it away. She drinks.

"You're drunk."

She mocks offense, pouts, decides the offense is real and glowers. Her face pulls in and lips push out, those eyes narrowed and swimming.

"You should go."

He gathers his things. There's not much to gather. He pauses at the door with his bag and his coat, his shirt untucked and the ends of his tie hanging from his collar. He looks her in the eye and offers a sad smile.

"Are you happy?" he asks.

"What does that matter?"

She ties his tie and straightens it, running one hand down his chest to flatten the fabric. The knot is tight against his throat as the door shuts behind him. A hot wind moves through the night. He doesn't know what day it is.

9.

The glow in the night is an oasis drawing the straggling derelicts in out of the dark. Florescent signs buzz. The chime marking his passage through the doorway comes at a delay seconds after the door has closed behind him.

There is a coffee poured as he sits and a nod of recognition or acknowledgement from Flo before she leaves a menu marked by greasy fingerprints to sit untouched before Charlie at his table. She doesn't speak and soon she has moved on.

There are only two of them playing cards, but others watch. Flo looks at them from the corners of her eyes as she passes but she does not talk to them. She does not offer to refill their drinks, coffees and waters, other things too murky or in glasses too opaque to be discerned. They sit across from each other at a table, the two players do, a man and his bearded lady. His wiry frame is covered by an olive drab work shirt with a pack of cigarettes in the right pocket that he touches when no one is looking but he does not smoke them. Tattooed black squares crisscross every inch of visible skin in a checkerboard of flesh and there are ten cards in his hand. Their game is a new mystery.

"Ace and two."

His tongue pokes from the corner of his mouth before his calm hand places cards facedown on the table. He looks the bearded lady in her bearded face.

"Shit."

His voice is a quiet thing with that one word, more a declaration than any kind of resignation. He drinks from a glass of room temperature water and stares across the table at the woman.

"You coming?"

He still looks at her but his words are for Charlie. The others at the table and some at tables nearby have quieted and strange eyes are turning to look. Charlie pulls a chair from his own table and sits between this man and his bearded lady. The others make room.

"There's plenty of food."

Charlie raises a hand and lowers his head. Thanks and no.

"I know you," says the checkered man.

Charlie points at the bearded lady.

"She knows me."

She shrugs, then nods. The checkered man shuffles cards, at first with one hand, then with two. The one hand is too showy. He's off the clock. He shuffles and speaks.

"You know how to play?"

The bearded lady answers for Charlie.

"He doesn't."

The checkered man shrugs.

"Okay."

He begins dealing out cards with long, agile fingers, a professional toss to the bearded lady, to Charlie, to himself. Charlie watches the cards make their circuit, not touching his as each is doled out.

"I need a ride."

"Yeah?"

"Where is the goon?"

The checkered man looks at the bearded lady. The bearded lady shrugs.

"In the hat," says Charlie. "The guy in the hat."

They both look at Charlie. He stares with expectation but they don't answer. He picks up his cards. The bearded lady laughs without obvious reason. Something unknown caught or a lost punchline found. She covers her mouth with the outstretched fingers of a pale, delicate hand. The white skin under her red whiskers gains a light blush of color.

The checkered man looks at her. A long moment passes by. He turns back to his cards.

"I used to play professionally. Only in the summers. I was a schoolteacher. Second grade. I lost two point one million in a hand once."

Pause.

"But it wasn't mine."

He exhales while he talks, every word a sigh. His eyebrows stand out against the black lines of his patchwork covering. His head is shaved, a thin sheen of blond fuzz sprouting on top.

Charlie stares at his cards with a profound bafflement.

"I don't know what I'm doing."

"Show me your hand."

Charlie holds up his cards for the checkered man.

"You didn't win."

He takes the cards and begins to shuffle again.

"It's a bad habit," says the bearded lady.

"What is?"

She gestures at the cards or at the table, at those seated there. Charlie speaks.

"I wouldn't call it a bad habit."

Her foot pushes against his under the table. Her hand on his thigh seems almost an afterthought. She looks with a distant interest at the cards as they are dealt. Somewhere the checkered man is talking.

"It's a habit. It's only bad when you lose."

But this is a lie. He feels guilt at his love of playing. He doesn't care about winning or losing. There is an anesthetic in the risk that he enjoys more than what comes at the end of the game. He looks at the cards as he deals them and Charlie hasn't been listening to what he's saying.

"Playing odds is a fine trade, but counting cards is a better one. I was banned from seventeen games before I quit."

His eyes blaze and there is a truth in this look like no other he has to offer.

"My deck is a special deck. Come play our game. Show me your palms."

But Charlie shows him nothing. The playing deck has the wrong number of cards and the faces are all wrong. This man has a secret and he likes himself too much. He ignores refusals and he asks the same questions over and over. His eyes dance in his head and he sways with drunken abandon in his seat. He shuffles the cards during play.

The conversation at the next table is about sales. Charlie understands. Something relatable. He cares or he used to. He looks over at a man with no neck and shoulders like a rhinoceros. The man drinks hot tea from a white cup and talks in animated zeal with a man in an old suit and round bifocals. They discuss output and cost and a former employee's fine, fine ass. A spindly man sits with them but says nothing. Sickly thin. A black t-shirt hangs from emaciated limbs. His bone fingers rest on a green notebook that sits on the table before him. He hasn't said a single word to anyone and he hasn't looked away from Charlie since Charlie sat down.

"You know where you're headed?" says the checkered man as he flips over a card. Charlie shrugs. The checkered man nods. "Good. That's where we're going."

———

The bearded lady fucks like she's angry. She uses fists and leaves bruises. Her whiskers tickle and Charlie has to keep his eyes open to keep from being repulsed. She calls him Sean and he doesn't correct her. Sometimes she calls him Sam.

"Do you have a phone?"

"What?"

"Give me your phone."

He pulls the cell from the pocket of his slacks. She dials with her eyes closed. She slows down and rocks but she does not stop moving. A clock on the wall is in the shape of a cat. The eyes move back and forth, slow, steady. The time is off by hours or days.

"Guess where I am, asshole."

She laughs into the phone. There is yelling on the other end, masculine and furious. She breathes into the phone and laughs again.

She puts a hand over the phone and looks down at Charlie. Her eyes never open.

"What's your name?"

"Charlie."

Into the phone again.

"Charlie knows how to fuck. What was your problem?"

The yelling gets louder. All gibberish and fire but it's clear just the same. She laughs again and hangs up.

It rings at once.

"Miss me?"

Her rhythm breaks for just a moment. Subtle but it's there.

"He wants to talk to you."

Charlie tries to get up but she puts the free hand on his chest and holds him down. She sets down the phone and he picks it up because he doesn't know what else to do.

"Hello?"

"Who is this?"

Drunken and southern but the accent sounds fake.

"This is Charlie."

She moves faster. Her mouth opens and tongue circles lips. She licks at the edges of her beard.

"Do I know you, Charlie?"

Her fingers wrap around his throat and he speaks in a wheeze.

"No."

"Well, Charlie, I hope she was worth it."

Charlie sucks in what little air can fight its way through those clutching fingers to fill his lungs but still he cannot speak.

"You're a dead man."

And that's when she comes.

———

Nervous grumblings of road underneath. A dozen buses marching in formation devour miles. Charlie is somewhere in the middle of their line if he is anywhere.

The back of the bust is her private suite. Large, stocked, a bathroom adjoining. The bathroom doesn't feel cramped at all. The room is filled with perfume and sex. A window looks out on the highway and night and a field that goes on for miles. Charlie pisses into a bleach-clean toilet with rosewater in the tank and he watches the dark empty play out on the other side of that window. The bus shudders and slows and someone up front yells words Charlie does not understand or even hear and the marching caravan trundles in slow determination past a burning wreck in a ditch. The long grasses of the field beyond have not yet caught and maybe someone somewhere is praying they never will but Charlie is not that someone. The fire means nothing to him.

The burning car sits alone and whoever was inside has left this place completely or have not left at all. They are not around. A child stands far off in the field with only the flickering light of the fire touching her face, the eyes in that face hidden in the dark but they do not watch the flames, instead looking into the bus and into Charlie as these things pass slowly by this little bit of ruin lost and left in the middle of nowhere.

Charlie wipes his eyes as he steps back into the bedroom proper. She has her back to him, her head down. She sits on the side of the bed and he doesn't know what to call her because he doesn't know her name. She whispers she's sorry, so sorry, over and over. He stands in the doorway and listens to the words. He doesn't know if she is saying this to Sean or to Sam. Maybe she's saying it to Charlie but he has already shut the door and there is no one there to hear.

———

The checkered man leans against the parked bus smoking and talking. Somewhere ahead someone changes a tire on a truck and the caravan sits idling, bored carnies mingling with their own cliques of freaks. Segregated oddities.

The starving man with the green notebook leans on a hand he holds against a step leading into one of the buses. That hand splayed out and fighting, his legs wobbly, his will steel. He looks at Charlie and hugs himself with his free arm, that green notebook pressed hard against chest, its secrets held tight.

The checkered man complains about his job but doesn't want to be anywhere else. He laughs and he breathes smoke into the night air. A chill wind blows but no one notices. Charlie offers him a dollar to bite the head off a chicken but he has no chicken and anyway he wouldn't give the man the dollar. The checkered man tells a story Charlie doesn't hear and when no one is looking he disappears completely.

10.

The sound of feet hitting pavement over and over is there long before Charlie looks up to see the man walking beside him. He was there long before Charlie heard the sound. This dreamer walks with his head down and his hands in his pockets to the elbows.

"There hasn't been a car through here in hours."

His voice is light and young. The whole world is ahead and all paths lead to exactly where he was going anyway.

Charlie walks with his chin up without reason. There is nothing ahead but road. A hill in the distance and on the other side who knows. A road, at least. There is always a road.

"They'll come. It's almost morning."

The dreamer looks at his feet but it isn't his feet he's seeing. His pupils are wide and his thoughts far away. Maybe remembering, maybe hoping. He's watching all the things the world could be if life would let it. He's thinking of a friend he misses or one he's never met. The corners of his mouth lift just so slightly sometimes but it never lasts. They're not all good dreams.

"Have you ever made anything?"

The dreamer sounds almost interested, but he remains in that far-off place and his words come from miles away.

"Lies," says Charlie.

"Lies are stories. Most men would be happy with that."

No crickets chirp, no night sounds in this place. The fields maintain their light sway but the world sits still.

"Where you headed?"

It's a pointless question and Charlie knows this even as he asks. He doesn't care and the dreamer doesn't care and they both walk because there is nothing else to do. A hand raises, a finger points, and that is all there is. The dreamer says things from time to time but they are fleeting and some of his words aren't meant for this place or for Charlie. His voice is refreshing in the vast stillness. It does not matter what he's saying, only that it is said. He doesn't speak like someone who wants to hear himself talk. When Charlie responds he gets no look from the dreamer. There are long pauses between words. He's not someone just waiting for his turn. Sometimes he doesn't talk for so long Charlie starts to think he's not going to say anything more at all.

Sometimes he does.

He looks off into some life only he can see, only he can know. A faint half smile rises, the knowing smirk of someone who can still look out and view the infinite.

"Some men, they go their whole lives and never make a thing."

———

He examines his phone with real attention for the first time in days. An unfamiliar voice screams its way through a voicemail. Charlie deletes it without listening. The itinerary has continued to update with names and dates that clash with the new reality. He dials Jess's number but hangs up before it rings.

———

A trucker with the baseball cap of a team that hasn't played in the city the hat claims for decades drops Charlie off somewhere between a city and the suburb it slowly swallows. The trucker nods and utters inaudible grunts or he coughs and Charlie shuts the door. A light turns green and cars honk at each other in beagle spasms.

Lines of dented cars with smashed windows and spray-painted slogans from angry misanthropes form a parking lot maze for Charlie to navigate with his bag held at his front for protection. The crunch of safety glass with every step gives away his position to anyone listening. For miles around enemies take up arms and smell the westerner sweat and listen to the crunch, crunch, crunch as he crosses the lot.

"Can I help you?"

There's no need for the tired man leaning against a pillar to wait for Charlie to open the door. The glass window circling the building's end has all been knocked out and someone has smeared mud or shit all along the handle of the metal frame that used to be the door.

Charlie speaks.

"I don't think you can. Can I help you?"

He doesn't try to hide the sarcasm in his voice. The tired man laughs as he looks around at the ruin of what used to be a car rental outlet. Major chain. Surely insured for double what the late-model liars with the unfathomably high miles on those engines are worth. Hulks aging too fast. The force that came through here did this man a favor. A fortuitous horror lies strewn about. These cars have lived too hard too fast. These whores of the road.

"Some kids."

It's all he says and it's all he has to. Maybe they believed in the things they wrote in fat yellow and red letters with condiments taken and bottles smashed that once inhabited the employee lounge refrigerator. Maybe they didn't believe those things written but felt like they should believe in something and didn't know how to aim that rage at something all their own or maybe they didn't have any rage but didn't know they have so many things they could be angry about that wouldn't ruin this guy's week, this middle-America schlub who'd rather be out painting annoying slogans for ideals he doesn't believe in on the walls of some city high-rise or some other bigger, brighter place in the world, ruining somebody higher on the ladder's week instead of having to put back together his own.

"How much do you want for the one with the sad face on the hood?"

———

The air slaps Charlie hard in the face as he guns the engine. There is an unsteady knock under the hood when he gets to third gear and he turns up the radio until he can't hear it. Wires hang loose where something should be but he doesn't know what. A cassette player hangs loose from the dash, a hack-job thrown together in minutes. The stereo was ripped out with an indelicate hand by the bored eco-kids. The schlub threw in the tape player for nothing.

Charlie runs red lights when no one is coming. He slows and looks but he does not stop. It's mid-morning at the least and the city is playful, flirty. People are out but not too many, people things happening inside buildings in every direction but the streets are halted, waiting. They'll be back soon.

He slows and parks on a street corner with healthy bright green grass and obsessively manicured hedges. A marquee reads sharp witticisms with religious themes and Charlie admires the shapely curves of the hedges while he stands for a minute doing nothing, just looking. The city sounds are heating up. There is a thing alive here. Breathing and honking and shouting and noises that don't belong but have no names to be touched or called. He takes them in and scrolls through the itinerary and he looks at the church and he smiles. He straightens his clothes just a little and hefts his bag in one hand. He opens the front door and feels that clean air wash over him.

———

Heads turn. Strangers fail to hide shocked eyes. A man in a cheap suit steps forward to head off the lumbering creature who has breached the sanctity of this holy place. His voice is crisp and professional but his face is stiff with alarm.

"Do you need some kind of help?"

Charlie goes directly into his pitch.

"I'm here to see the pastor. I have an appointment."

This is as far as he gets. The man in the cheap suit takes Charlie by the wrist and attempts to guide him to one of the many empty pews. The huddled souls from which the man appeared only watch, unsure just what has come into their midst.

"Are you hungry? We have cans from the food drive. Have a seat."

Charlie stops moving. His arm is hauled forward and the man doesn't notice until he reaches the end of his tether. Charlie pulls his arm away and reaches into his bag.

"I have an appointment."

He holds up a book so all eyes can see. The crowd remains unchanged. The man in the cheap suit cocks his head to the side, eyebrows arching as uncertainty sets in.

"What are you here about?"

Charlie straightens his tie. He wants to shoot his cuffs but he does not do this.

"I'm here to see the pastor."

The man in the cheap suit takes Charlie into a back office in which a gentle old man sits reading a paperback. He looks up and nods and they shake hands. The old man goes back to his paperback while the man in the cheap suit takes the reins once more. Charlie runs through the scripted talk with forced aspect that's more grimace than smile. The standard questions are asked and answered and the man in the cheap suit is too professional to comment on Charlie's looks, the bedraggled urchin from whom he's purchasing bibles.

"You were supposed to be here last week."

Charlie nods his playful agreement.

"Everything's backed up, someone should've called about this. The website's down but you can make the check out to me and we'll get you fixed up."

All that's left is paperwork and smiles and the practiced banter of the shilling trade. A check changes hands. The old man looks up once more from his paperback.

"Give us a minute."

The man in the cheap suit steps into the hall without a word. The old man marks his page with his finger.

"You can stay here. You don't have to go."

Charlie looks at the door, looks at the chair across from the old man.

"Sit a minute."

The sound the chair makes as it scrapes across the uncarpeted floor is jarring in the quiet of the room. The old man seems not to notice. Charlie sinks into the chair with the glum air of a chastised child.

"You should stay."

"Why?"

The old man nods as if this is all the answer either man needs.

"What is it you're after?" asks the old man.

"I don't understand the question."

"A fool would offer you some kind of cautionary tale, a lot of words and a moral. You'd nod, and when it's over you'd thank them, and nothing would change. They'd feel better and you, you would feel nothing. I am no fool, sir. You won't find what you're after. It may exist and it may not, but you won't find it doing this."

Charlie's face is stone.

"What am I after?"

"Exactly."

The gathered faces in the main foyer don't turn as Charlie moves past them, skirting the edge of their huddled conclave. The man in the cheap suit trails at his heels, a disinterested chatter leaking from his mouth. Once past the group he puts a hand out to pause Charlie's escape. The two men stop. The man in the cheap suit shudders, shaking loose whatever statement he grasps for. He leans away as if repulsed by the creature standing before him. He speaks.

"You don't look well."

Charlie nods and he thanks the man in the cheap suit as he makes his way to the door.

———

He's looking at himself in the car's side mirror when a man asks for a ride. Charlie tears his attention from the lines in his own face, the deepening wells of purple below wide eyes with earnest reluctance. The man nods like he's already gotten a yes. He offers money for the ride but Charlie doesn't take it. He says his name but Charlie couldn't care less. Something official. One of those names with an overbearing initial in the middle, that initial a relic from some other lifetime. He laughs every few seconds for the first twenty miles. Charlie doesn't ask for the man's story and it's some time before the man tells it.

"She had me declared dead three weeks ago."

He shakes a pack of off-brand cigarettes from a pocket and lowers his head in prayer as he holds it out before him.

"Mind if I smoke?"

Charlie puts up a hand. No thanks. Go ahead. He lights up with a small wooden match and blows it out with a gentle breath. He puts the match in a coat pocket and pats it just once.

"You think she had it planned out?"

Charlie doesn't commit to answering. The dead man doesn't seem to mind.

"I think she had it planned out. My passport, my papers, my money, anything that could give me a fighting chance. She left the hotel with everything. It wasn't an accident. This was no whim."

He smokes and watches the road and Charlie now wants a cigarette. He cracks the window and the dead man ashes out through the inch of open space at the top of his. He taps the cigarette out in the hole that used to be the ashtray before whoever ripped it out. He puts the stub in his pocket.

"You know in most states that takes seven years? To legally declare somebody dead. Seven years. Lucky me, I come from one of those ones who bumped it down to five."

He has no luggage and his clothes are old, worn. Thick and patched and he hasn't shaved in weeks. His hair stands in uncaring tufts and he laughs again.

"But you know what pisses me off? You know what really makes the whole thing one of those stories you shake your head over? Just going, 'I don't fucking believe the brass fucking balls on this lady.' I was happy. I could've gone the rest of my life being dead and it would've been fine. She got the money, great. I honestly could not care. And now, now she sends somebody looking and just that fast it's phone calls and how much she missed me, how hard it's all been on her. On her."

"So why come back now?," asks Charlie in a conversational voice that sounds too much like his salesman tone. "So she found you, so what. Stay dead. You won't be any happier going back to confront her now."

"Oh, I'm not going to be confronting anybody. When I get there I'm going to marry her again."

Charlie pays for the room because he thinks the dead man is lying when he says he has money. The only empty room is a double. A clerk says this and other things that hold the stink of lies but there is a thick, wet plop every time the man blinks and Charlie no longer has the strength to argue.

The stairs are carpeted with late-'70s magenta. A chandelier once hung overhead but is now only a circle of holes drilled in the stained veneer. The sound of fucking or fighting grumbles behind every wall and every door is locked. The rates aren't hourly but someday they will be. No one will ever write a book of the memories of this place but it has so many stories to tell. Maybe it wants to forget.

The room smells like cleaning solutions. The television is pay only. Charlie hugs his bag to his body and he is asleep in moments. He wakes up once or twice to hear the dead man's shouts as he growls into the room's only phone. Maybe those shouts are made only to the room, maybe into the dead man's own head. But on the phone or in the room or in his own head, wherever that shouting is meant to be going there is no one listening.

———

An indolent light spills across the coverlet in yellow and pointless sprawl. It paws at the dark like a feeble teenager but illuminates little and gives nothing. The streetlight maintains a firm, unending buzz that rattles the window in its frame. Charlie rolls over and looks at that light spilling in, a flickering off and on and that angry buzz, a million bees trapped inside a bowl of sodium gas attached to a pole on the other side of that window. He closes his eyes and that buzz grows stronger, so strong he almost doesn't hear the closet door groan on its hinges as it opens with aching slowness. Eyes squeeze tighter and he pulls the blanket higher, only chin peeking over the top and fingers clamped at the edge.

A weight presses at the edge of the bed, something light but there.

"Hello, Charlie."

His eyelids are so tight it hurts his head. So tight he has to open them or risk bursting eyeballs in their sockets, the jellied goop he sees through running down his cheeks like the tears of a bad dream.

Someone is there.

The dark of the room hides him, it, that weak yellow light hinting more than showing, the black of night giving him, it, sanctuary. It rests on the edge of the bed, leans more than sits. Its frame is thin, too thin, bones and flesh and cloth and darkness. Yellow fingers protrude from the edge of dark sleeves that quickly disappear into the night. The buzz hides the sound of its thoughts and the light blinks off and on, off and on, making this phantom thing into a stop-motion figure, jerkily moving when it moves at all.

"Where are you going, Charlie?" he or it asks, but Charlie doesn't say anything. He doesn't say anything because the streetlight blinks off and does not come back and the buzz cries out with all its fury and anguish before ending its song altogether and his eyes open wide to find a soft blue light bathing the room through open blinds and there is no one sitting on the bed but Charlie as he breathes in, out, in, filling lungs with stale motel air.

He wipes sleep from eyes and looks out the room's window. There is no sodium light on the other side, no pole, no bees buzzing by the million. Before he rolls back over, before he pulls the covers back over his body, before he buries his face in the pillow and forgets all the rights he's never wronged, all the worlds he's never saved, all the sins of this life and others, before any of that, he pushes closed the closet door.

———

There is a room service tray in the room. The sun is hiding on the other side of a curtain but it is up and alive out there someplace. Warm and bright. A half a pot of coffee is getting cold on that tray. There is only one cup. Charlie is the only person in the room. He marvels at the newfound knowledge that shitholes like this have room service.

The sample bag is still in Charlie's arms and he hesitates to let go. He does but he looks over at where it sits several times as he pours a cup of tepid coffee and drinks it in a gulp. It's somehow watered down and bitter at the same time. He pours another cup and look over at his bag.

The sun runs faint fingers across his skin as he walks across the street to the car. The door is unlocked and there is nothing inside to steal. He jams hands in pockets for the keys but they are in the ignition. He crosses back to the motel.

There is a light music coming from a room on the first floor, something contemporary and uninspired. The vocals are layered and trip over themselves when they are doing anything more than humming absently in kindergarten lilts.

"I want the room for another day."

The same clerk from last night reads a paper from weeks ago. There is a clown on the front page but the headline is full of enigmatic wordplay that is immediately ignored. The smaller stories are all bad news. He folds it neatly but doesn't set the paper down, it suspended in air between hands shaky from God knows how many days awake. He blinks fat, wet plops but says nothing.

"Did the guy I came in with leave already?"

And he does set that paper down. He folds the already folded sheet in half and nudges it until it is square with the nub of counter he sits at, watching the world go by outside.

"What guy?"

11.

"I'm going to win the lottery tonight. How much you wanna bet I do?"

The sunken pits in his skull are eyes. His clothes look hand-sewn and old. He wears a vest under a thick coat and no tie. That faint smell is something like mildew, sharp but distant. Greasy hair shines in the glow of the overheads. The fingers of his left hand tap one after another, slow, monotonous. His right hand does nothing.

"You wanna play?"

Charlie doesn't want to play. He's had enough of gambling. A deck of cards sits uncut and untouched between the man's two hands, the one tapping that slow tap, the other just sitting, waiting. The tapping hand is missing one finger and the sequence is awkward. Tap, tap . . . tap. The dark holes in his face are turned to front, the eyes inside watching with calculating interest. The stakes are anybody's guess. The game is foggy and uncertain.

"Someone asked me if I wanted to play once," says the gambler.

Through the muted window Charlie watches cars pass in the streets. There are so many. It must be a Friday night or a holiday. A man on the sidewalk puts his arm around a woman's waist and whispers something into an ear with holes but no earrings. She laughs. Somewhere on the other side of this scene and that traffic is a motel. The same clerk sits at the same counter reading the same news over and over and talking quietly in an empty room.

"And did you?" says Charlie without turning to the man sitting across from him. They sit at a round table in a quiet bar in some city Charlie will never pass through again.

"For awhile."

The man's face is a mask that offers up nothing. A placid mouth, lips slightly parted and a wall of square teeth hinted at but not seen fully. His breathing is even, bored. Professionally serene.

"Are you gonna deal those?"

Maybe his eyes look at the cards but nothing moves and Charlie doesn't know for sure.

"This is a deck of fifty-one."

"Like in the song," says Charlie, not sure if it's a joke, or if it is why he bothers. And the man is lying. That deck has a lot more than fifty-one.

"What song?"

Charlie doesn't say anything and that hand goes on tapping. The man lets it for a while and Charlie watches the finely manicured nails as they connect with the lacquered tabletop. Those nails are the only thing maintained on his person, neat and out of place.

"It doesn't matter. I play other games now. I just keep the cards to remind me."

There are doors on every wall and a hallway next to a narrow spine of stairs but only the door to the outside goes anywhere. Charlie looks to each of these and pretends he's not studying the man on the other side of the table. He goes on tap, tap . . . tapping and showing nothing.

Talk is small and meaningless and it goes on for an extravagant length of the night. The gambler says nothing but says it slowly and for as long as he likes, his face slack and his mouth moving only when it must. A dark stain slowly spreads on the front of his vest, obscured at first by the edges of his coat and then more visible as his story goes on. He was in a game once a long time ago. A man had a gun and a single shot was fired and someone's honor was first called into question and then rendered immaterial with the introduction of the bullet and the game went on but one man could not play. A stranger played his hand and a life's work was lost in a night. He says some of this and he says other things and Charlie reads what he wants but the gambler offers very little, that stony, dead face. That card-player face.

A crash echoes off the walls as metal hits metal outside in a pounding wreck of someone's ride home and paintings rattle in their frames in the soiled little barroom but the man across from Charlie doesn't flinch and he does not shake. He does not waver and he goes on playing his game.

Charlie leaves the table. He wants no part of this game.

———

Sinister seems melodramatic but it is the first word that comes to mind when a man walks in off that dusty sidewalk leading in from the interstate. The shadows that cover the better part of his long form are real or make-believe, sometimes both, cloth suggestions of a traveling darkness and the pale form underneath. His hat was maybe once a slouch but has since taken its look from its namesake, the wide brim hanging low like a rain hat or some shrugging, beaten animal. A long black coat drags along the ground but he does not notice. Water runs from the arms and down the sides but outside the sky is a calm, lackadaisical blue. Only at this very moment does Charlie start to wonder how many days he's been in this place, this nameless town along the interstate.

The man looks over his shoulder as he sits down next to Charlie. His face is unremarkable and unfamiliar and will not be quite remembered even minutes from now. The clerk at the desk turns a page on his paper and sees neither of these strangers. This man does not remove his hat and he does not remove his coat. His boots are hard-worn leather with thick, cracked soles. Mud seeps from the lines that crisscross their patchy surface every time he moves.

"Some places are just never quiet."

He raises a hand to the clerk but this does nothing and he pulls a bright, polished flask from beneath his coat. He offers it to Charlie. Charlie does not move and the man unscrews the top slowly. He drinks and puts it away.

"All places are like this," says the man. "So much noise."

There is a second of pause in which the man might be done, but in time he finds his voice.

"You're going west."

Another quick drink and a throaty sigh and he speaks again.

"Storm's heading east. Just behind me if it's not here already."

Charlie reaches down with one hand to touch the bag sitting next to his chair like an arcane charm against the terrors of the wretched. He pulls the bag closer so it touches his leg and leans forward until the table is pressed hard against ribs.

"Do you know me?" Charlie asks with dry wisps of words.

The sound of the man's tongue is an audible thing as it rakes slowly along lips like a man who has been lost in the desert for days. That pink protrusion is a fat, crawling thing.

"What's in the bag?"

Charlie doesn't look down but his leg pushes against it, a light touch to reassure. It's still there. He brushes against it again and he will several more times before he is sure.

"God is in that bag."

He opens the sample case with one hand to give this man God, but all the things inside are tricks and feints, glamours for the mind. The man smiles.

"It's okay. I have one already."

Something bubbles in his throat and he barks shaky coughs into a wet hand before he jumps tracks on the subject at hand.

"You remind me of someone."

The man leans against the table and his hunger comes off in waves. His hands are flat on the table, fingers spread like the eager paws of a child. Those hands leave wet spots spreading out from fingers that vibrate with energy on the old wood of the tabletop.

"You have the stink of a saint."

The brown paneling of an antique station wagon pulls to a stop outside the door leading into the front room of the motel. Other cars pass at a leisurely pace, no real hurry, individuals or groups, a family, ones and twos, sometimes whole carloads. Sometimes caravans.

Most are heading east.

Someone in that station wagon turns their face in a slow pull of tendons and flesh to look through their window, to look through that door, to look into this room at Charlie sitting at this table, leaning hard, hands squeezed into fists and heart punching blood through veins. The face in that car looks but Charlie cannot look back, a glaring light on that window dazzling sight and muddying the face of whoever hides on the other side.

They sit there for a long time. Just looking.

The man across from Charlie pushes the table, not hard but hard enough. Hard enough to jolt. A single eye turns their way from the clerk at the counter. He ruffles his paper and this is all.

"There is a man upstairs slowly bleeding into a bathtub while twenty-five gallons of water cools around his pruning skin. There are other men like you in this world. Many men, but less every day. A storm is washing across the sands."

He hits the table with his pelvis and leans, almost bends over its surface, conspiring, the pale of his skin harsh against the minimal light of the room. His skin is dripping with a slick, oily water but his lips are cracked and peeling.

"They'll come for you."

This mad prophet takes his hat in hand and wipes one coat sleeve across his forehead as he stands. The motion obscures his whole head for a moment and Charlie never sees what hides underneath that hat. The clerk puts his paper in front of his face and quietly disappears forever.

The prophet puts the hat back on and looks down at Charlie, still leaning hard against the table. A long black hardtop stops in the street where the station wagon was a moment ago. The other car is nowhere to be seen and Charlie feels like this should matter but it doesn't. This other car, this throwback with whitewalls and the rumbling giant under the hood, it idles and it growls and it waits and it waits. The man looking down at Charlie stays just a moment longer and then turns. A trail of wet footprints follows him out the door and into the world. For just a moment the cool black steel of a classic car door is open and a long face is looking out with a fine hat above. A driver's cap, one of those old ones with the partitions. A Gatsby. A splintered cigar hangs from the vaguely pink lips of the monster looking out and maybe, maybe he reaches up a huge hand with long, bony fingers to tip that hat but then the door is closed and the beast gives one growl and then a snarl and then they, all of them, are gone.

The rain begins almost at once.

———

The stairs have a sticky quality to them. The lighting has changed but not in any definable way. Different is good enough. Different is all that matters.

There is the meek clap of a single gunshot from somewhere ahead and around a corner as Charlie climbs one step at a time. Any of the doors lining the hallway could hide that sound and the little piece of the world that owns it but he sets his bag on the floor in front of the correct one and closes eyes as he puts a hand on the door's tarnished brass knob. Its round shell is cool to the touch and just slightly rough, years upon years of rust leaving a muddy smear of metal on his palm.

The room's bed is unwrinkled and immaculate and there is a bible by the phone. A sliver of dark stands visible in the crack of an open closet doorway. This he looks away from at once. A lock hides the television's secrets and there is one bag in the room. Save the one bag the room has the look of a maiden, a thing untouched for a very long time or never at all.

The bathroom light is on.

Charlie pushes the door wide but doesn't go in. The room feels cold but there is a memory of warmth here. The body in the water stares with wide, unknowing eyes at a spot in the corner but when Charlie looks that way there is nothing there. The dead man in the tub is a stranger and his death means nothing to Charlie. The water is a scarlet wash but there are no wounds on the body. Charlie does not bother with a meticulous examination or even enter the room. There are no weapons, no razors or broken curios with jagged grins, no gun here. No note left to be found by Charlie or anyone else.

There is no one in the room.

Charlie stands by the bag sitting on the floor for a moment. The latch on top is affixed but not locked. He reaches down but stops several inches short, just standing there, one arm hanging low, fingers arched, poised to scrabble at that latch, to cleave it in two, to tear out its miles of guts and know all its stories.

Through the doorway leading to the hallway sits Charlie's own bag, just over the precipice, sitting. Waiting.

He stands up straight and turns to the bedside table. The phone and the bible. He touches the cover of that bible, eons of infinite influence wrapped in rough acreage and a cheap stamp with the name of a motel on the flap.

He moves to his bag but does not leave the room as he bends to open its latch and take out one of the books stashed there. He doesn't bother latching it back as he moves into the bathroom. There is still nothing in the empty spot where those eyes conduct a search both endless and pointless. Charlie takes a ropey wet arm and wraps it around the book and steps back a moment. He steps close again and fumbles in first one pocket and then another and then the first again and comes out with a handful of change both foreign and otherwise. He closes each of those empty eyes before setting a penny on first one and then the other. He doesn't say a prayer and he's sure the dead man understands.

———

The traffic in the street goes both directions once more and Charlie tells himself it's about even, that the cars and trucks and vans and freights going east aren't double or maybe even triple that of the westbound travelers. He tells himself the man in the slouch hat and the wet coat was a fool with flighty stories made to spook children with their vague hints and aggressive intensities. He looks up into the black clouds directly above, at the patches of blue in front and behind, really every direction, any direction, the storm only here, right here. He looks at this only a moment before he raps the back of his hand on the door of the little wounded car with the spray-painted hood and dented husk he's taken possession of for the time being.

"Can I help you?" says Charlie in an almost bored voice.

The kid inside looks up with panic in his muted pink eyes. His fingers stay where they are on the frayed wires of the primeval cassette player. A line of snot runs from one pasty nostril. His age is an unknowable thing, his bone-white skin free of wrinkles and meaning. He could be twenty or fifty and Charlie would nod agreeably if told either. The kid's hair is a naked yellow if it is any color at all. His words are a cough and he repeats them over and over.

"Help me," he says. "I'm sick."

12.

How Charlie has found himself in the car with this stranger, he does not know for sure. The sickly kid says little and Charlie doesn't offer him a ride but he doesn't tell the kid to leave and when Charlie looks over as the highway is swallowed underneath ever more balding tires the kid sits in the passenger bucket with a distant, faintly dreamy frown on mild pink lips that speak silent words to no one. He raises a cold blue handkerchief to the tiny bulb of his nose and dabs at the milk skin underneath. The kerchief is dark and wet and what soaks its pregnant bowels is obscured by the cloth but the smell of blood and sick is clear in the thin air of the car.

"I'm not an albino."

His eyes are straight ahead. They dart Charlie's way but he doesn't turn. He dabs at that spot under his nose, a smear of rust left behind that he lightly touches over and over but never fully erases.

"I'm not asking."

Charlie doesn't look at him either but he sees him just the same. Something like panic, those eyes that can't sit still, that stink of something wrong inside forcing its way out through the nose, through the mouth, through every pore until the thing wrong inside is the thing wrong outside and they're all one and the same, this big pale ball of wrong erupting blood and mucus maybe not here, maybe not in the passenger bucket but somewhere, someplace soon.

Charlie offers a tissue but of course the plagued kid doesn't take it. He has his dark blue sponge of sick.

Charlie doesn't have a tissue anyway.

"Are you a religious man?" says the plague between sniffles. Between dabs.

"Something like that."

Dab. Sniffle.

"Something like that, huh. I like that. I think that's the right answer."

Sniffle. Sniffle. Dab. He seems more sure of himself. He nods and repeats.

"That's the right answer. I'm something like that, too. Something like a religious man. I'm being . . ."

The next words come out but they're shattered by violent coughs that ruin any meaning they have. This fit goes on for half a minute, another half just remembering what it's like to breathe normal breaths, a faint sadness at what it may have been like to breathe healthy ones once upon a time and then he's speaking again.

"I'm being punished by God."

The road bends and crawls and cars pass by going the other direction or careening into the other lane to pass by at teeth grinding speeds, some going somewhere, some going nowhere but all going fast.

"You think so?"

Sniffle.

"I know so."

The tinny pitch of a forgotten phone's forlorn ring issues just once from the recesses of Charlie's bag and then falls quiet. The plague doesn't look at the bag. He doesn't look around at all and the interruption goes unnoticed. A hand folds the kerchief over and dabs with a new spot, never blowing the nose, only touching lightly to that place under each nostril, over and over, like a machine, broken, its use long since forgotten but still the works of its gears endlessly turning with no notion of their futility.

"Wouldn't you punish something like me if you were God?"

Charlie says nothing and the plague expects just this.

"God made Man in His image, isn't that the joke? God made this flabby pink ball of meat to go around making wonderful mistakes as long as it can, picking flowers and impregnating Dorothy whoever down at the local whatever and ain't life grand . . ."

Cough.

"But God didn't make me in His image. Maybe . . . maybe God didn't make me at all. This offense in His eye. This abomination."

He sneezes a ball of snot and blood onto the passenger side of the windshield and Charlie doesn't look over. The plague dabs and he sniffles and pretty soon the sound of his breathing is covered by the sound of his sobbing and still Charlie doesn't look over. A car swerves into the other lane at eighty or ninety or some screaming fury speed and maybe it's a station wagon with wood paneling or maybe it's not but its driver doesn't look and the face of that driver is familiar, a pretty face, the kind of face a person could love if they knew it long enough, well enough. But that too is a lie. A person doesn't need to know that face to love it, the warmth of the person it belongs to written all over it in ways felt but never recognized enough to put to words; the kindness of the line of the jaw, the heart of the way the eyes are set, the purity of soul in the curve of the nose and of course that one beautiful wrinkle. All of these things going by at eighty or ninety if they were ever there at all.

After awhile Charlie speaks.
"All of us, we're all abominations."

———

The engine hums softly, its mantra all modern and bored. The aging fluorescents of the twenty-four-hour grocery mart pulsate to a rhythm only they know, almost chastising in their intensity. Charlie runs hands over the steering wheel and leans against the seat's headrest. The night is black and goes on forever. The parking lot is empty except for Charlie and a beater of an elder vintage sitting locked and cold in a corner spot at the unlit edge of the macadam. A bird, something oily blue and incongruous at this hour sits on the cement hump of a parking curb, watching, watching.

The inside of the store is heaven white through wide robot doors that wait to slide open at the approach of the next saint. The albino walks down aisle after aisle touching items but not picking them up. More white, more ghostly under the lights in that store burning holes in the glass with their pale ferocity.

The engine idles, lulling, sweet gasoline nothings. The bird, a grackle or a crow or some other dark beast disinterested in most delights of this world, steps stocky steps along the curb, a little dance from foot to foot and always it watches with huge empty eyes and so does Charlie.

The engine idles and then it doesn't as he turns the key hard, a scream of steel somewhere in the engine the only response. He shuts off the car and he slams the door with the keys still in it as if daring the bird, but that slick oil blue doesn't flinch and it doesn't fly away.

———

There is no overhead speaker leaking a tinny version of some vaguely remembered '70s hit and this is only the first thing that is wrong as the silent robot doors squeeze shut behind Charlie's trespass. A tired man with enough mustache for two stares ineffectively at a bottle of Maalox. Tie hangs loose around thick neck, suit coat probably left in an office full of invoices for something someone doesn't need. That mustache wobbles in a fair Yosemite Sam as he speaks quiet words to the bottle on the shelf. Charlie doesn't get close enough to hear the words and he doesn't need to. Ingredients and directions. The man reads each twice. Three times. Charlie moves to another aisle.

A kid with wild curls reaching to any direction at all above a face uninterested in excitement sits on a stool pointing a laser price gun at various products. Bang, you're a buck and a half. He doesn't take notice of Charlie until he is within striking distance and by then it's too late to run.

"You don't buy into time travel, do you?"

Charlie manhandles a can of creamed corn and pretends not to hear.

"That's okay, neither do I. Cruel men from dead futures come here to earn small fortunes making sure people like you and me don't believe in things like time travel."

He points his laser gun at Charlie and pulls the trigger. Nothing happens.

"You dress like a preacher."

Charlie sets down his sample case to button his top button, the t-shirt underneath all but hidden. He adjusts his tie but it remains jutting at its inelegant slant. He doesn't let go of the corn. The boy looks him over, the price gun forgotten and lame in a swinging arm by his side. The boy has a wide, lazy grin and knowing eyes that look unhurried at whatever they find.

"How long have you worked here?" asks Charlie without turning his face from the can of corn.

"All my life."

Charlie takes his eyes from the can but doesn't set it down. He holds it up in front of his eyes and turns to the kid.

"How long is that?"

The gun is remembered as he brings that arm up to point at Charlie, the can shielding its menace.

"It's forever, man."

Bang.

———

A piercing whoop descends to impact over and over and the robot doors shut tight but Charlie stands unconcerned at the checkout as the albino and whatever he stole disappears in the darkness of the parking lot. The kid mutters *shit* to no one in particular but doesn't call the cops and doesn't look anything but worn. His eyes don't dart and they don't widen. It's not sleepy but something like it. Old but that's not it either. He doesn't run the water and crackers across the reader on the register, instead leaves the counter altogether. Charlie follows him with eyes but doesn't move. In a minute the alarm stops and he comes back to stand in the same spot he left. He looks Charlie in the face with those tired eyes. Time passes.

"You're still here?"

Charlie takes his things and places them with earnest delicacy inside his bag. He carefully shuts and clasps it before walking out through the robot doors without paying.

The night is crisp but the air is clean. The bird is no longer on the parking curb and something loosens inside Charlie at this. A generously mustached man stands on the sidewalk with a tie hanging limp around his neck and a bottle of Maalox in hand that he tips to his mouth every few seconds. After a moment he points with the bottle at the empty place where Charlie's beaten former rental used to be.

"A ghost came out and ran off with your car."

Charlie unclasps his bag and takes out a bottle of water. He drinks from it as he looks out at the empty acres of concrete that lay ahead.

"Of course he did."

———

Thumbs up and out and no one stops. A cop slows and eyes and Charlie smiles and bows and the cop drives on. The morning becomes the day and Charlie's insides are tightened by hunger's twisting fingers. Strangers do not look at him as he passes and he surely must smell by now. He gives pleasant anythings to those who will look him in the eye. Some return kind words, others do not.

A man with the beard Charlie will soon have glares through sly lids from across the street. He spots the bearded man long before he comes over. The bearded man was there long before he was spotted.

"You eat?"

Charlie does or he has, the question is ambiguous. Charlie only nods.

"Come on."

He walks away and Charlie follows. Around a corner and up to a small square of building with a window on one side and a door on the other. A kind woman, young and far too naïve, waves with genuine cheer as the bearded man steps up. He orders a baked potato and a beer and Charlie orders the same.

"You some kind of salesman?"

His squinting glare falls on Charlie's sample case as Charlie takes a seat at what was once a white picnic table. The paint is not just chipped but pealing in long strips in some places and someone has tried to cover this with spray paint in others. It hasn't worked. There is another table set nearby with no paint on it at all. Gray stain of old wood. Names of the dead are carved in its surface but Charlie cannot see this from here. These two tables and the square food stand are all that inhabit a grassy vacant lot in what is otherwise an industrial landscape.

"Here."

Charlie takes a book from his bag and hands it to the bearded man. The man wipes his hand on a thick brown work shirt that is only partly buttoned. He looks more like something inhabiting ancient caves and feeding on his finds in cold forests than a member of this society or any other. He looks at the book like its some unrecognizable relic from a world that has yet to exist. Maybe it is.

The woman steps from her square kitchen hive and sets two thick paper plates on the leprous table. A fat bulb of potato sits in the center of a pool of congealing gravy. A steamed green pile of indistinct vegetable lies off to one side. The beer is in a sweaty glass bottle. The label shows the gleaming teeth of a smiling German woman but no writing. Lederhosen, frilly and absurd. She holds a bottle with the same label. Picture in picture until the end of time.

The bearded man sets the book aside as he digs into his food with plastic utensils, but it never fully leaves his attention. His gaze creeps over when it forgets not to.

He does not open the book.

"Who?"

Less a word than a noise. A greasy young man with greasy long hair sits down next to Charlie. He takes a pocketknife from some inner chamber of the thick brown coat that hangs on his skinny shoulders and cuts a hunk from the potato on Charlie's plate. Greasy fingers take the hunk and jam it into his grimy face. He looks at Charlie and he looks at the bearded man and he looks at Charlie again and he chews potato and grease.

"Who the fuck are you?"

The bearded man puts down a fat slab of potato dripping gravy speared on the end of a fork he holds in a fist. He holds a plastic knife in the other fist. It trembles.

"He gave me a book."

The little one laughs. Potato spills out of his mouth and onto his lap. He doesn't notice. Charlie puts his fork down and reaches for the bag under the bench.

"You can't get nothin' for a book."

He goes on laughing. The bearded man, he doesn't laugh. Maybe he remembers the fork is only plastic. He puts it down on the bare face of the table and reaches behind his back.

And Charlie stands up.

Neither of these savages looks his way. Neither looks away from the other.

"He gave me a book," the bearded man repeats, and Charlie is off and around the corner and back the way he came before another word is spoken. The last thing he sees is the wide eyes of the innocent girl in the little square of kitchen.

He does not stop to save her.

———

"Put yer goddamn thumb down. You're embarrassing me."

Wraparound shades, futuristic and frightening to look at. He leans all the way out the window of the subcompact with the flames on the side and a jagged hole cut in the hood to let out what may be a completely unnecessary series of pipes.

He doesn't ask where Charlie is going. Charlie sits in the passenger seat without the seatbelt on just in case. A disembodied bell chimes on the dash every half minute or so. The engine rumbles like a car twice its size. When the man presses the gas Charlie can hear its knowing anger.

He slows at certain intersections. His head cranes around in hydraulic jerks. Scanning. Mutters words Charlie doesn't catch, then repeats so he can.

"You see those motherfuckers?"

Charlie rolls down the window but this doesn't help.

"Which ones?"

The car speeds up and the man watches the road for a few blocks. The radio is on but too low to hear. He changes stations but does not turn it up.

"The two unruly heathens. You've got their smell all on you."

He turns his face to Charlie but the eyes are hidden behind those wide slick mirrors and all Charlie sees is himself. The man grins as he sets a handgun on the console between he and Charlie and he does not watch the road. The gun is a small dull black thing with no writing stamped in its side.

"Don't worry, I won't tell."

He could mean anything by this and Charlie does not bother to question. Charlie stares at the mirror of the man's eyes and the car slowly rolls to a stop. A light turns red almost directly above and in every direction there are cars suddenly filled with the anger of the great unwashed. An aging Volkswagen minibus pulls up to the bumper of the little subcompact and begins honking a jittery song of fury. The minibus is painted in a loose interpretation of the Scooby Doo van colors. The off-brand Mystery Machine is driven by a fat man with long black hair who slams a fat hairy fist into his steering wheel over and over again but his horn is weak and only barks those tinny froths.

A light turns green. Another turns red.

"I haven't seen anyone like that."

The look of almost glee on the man's face evaporates and he seems only confused. A hand pulls a card from the blind and presses it into Charlie's damp palm. The writing is textured. Charlie reads what it has to say but the words are vague and mean nothing to him. Turns it over. An address on the back and nothing more. Charlie tries to hand it back but the man puts up a hand and leans away until his head is sticking out the other window.

"Use it if you change your mind. There are a lot of bad people in the world."

He flashes his happy face one more time and guns the engine.

A light turns red.

———

The rumble of a foreign subcompact with a fiery disposition is audible for blocks until finally it is not and only then does Charlie set the bag down and spit in his palm. He uses that hand to straighten his hair, feels the natural part from one angle and does his best to sculpt presentability out of the sweaty wreck that he is. He runs a finger along teeth and spits in the street. He remembers the toothbrush in the bag and repeats the process. He turns his back to the building he's come to and spits in the street again. A car passes filled with laughing children and he forgives them for laughing at this lost and dirty urchin. There but for the grace of God.

A broad but short marquee is lit by a line of small yellow bulbs despite the afternoon sun making this pointless. Block letters spell out *JESUS IS A FRIEND OF SINNERS* in a three-line parable whose plot could be epic or sarcastic. Charlie doesn't check the itinerary. It doesn't matter anymore. He licks his lips as he steps through a front door propped open with a rubber stop. The interior is dim, white light filtering through stained-glass scenes. A man in a gray shirt, with a broom in hands, looks out of the shadows and stops his idle back-and-forth sweep. He does not speak, only turns and leaves the large chapel through an unlit side hallway. Charlie runs a free hand through hair, remembers the part, sets the bag down to rebuild it from scratch. It takes too long.

A man with glasses on his nose and curly graying hair steps out of the darkness of the hall. His hands dangle in the pockets of slacks pressed but still wrinkled. Shirt but no jacket. Suspenders. Tie, expensive, solid reserved colors. Grandfatherly but this is all facade. There is something knowing and sinister in that face. Observant beyond the point of okay. Aware.

"Lost your way?"

Charlie picks up the bag with one hand and walks forward with the other stretched before him.

"I'm looking for the man in charge."

Whatever sales pitch, whatever name Charlie was about to give, whatever song and dance was about to twirl its way out of his mouth, it is wiped away by the look in this man's eyes. The lying smile on Charlie's face dies a slow but definitive death. The hand slowly falls. Maybe it gives a twitch or two but then it just hangs there, dead and worthless.

"I'll bet you are."

A chill rides its way down Charlie's back and squeezes muscles rigor mortis tight. Some arcane notion of self-preservation screams out to beat this amiable apparition to a pool of floundering mess in the floor and flee to a mountain cave where all will be well, all will be safe, but the rational side cowed by too many pseudo-civilized generations ignoring a survival imperative creeps out to tell Charlie the situation is okay, things are in control, normal, normal, normal.

And he sees all this.

And he doesn't care. It is beneath his interest. Charlie is beneath his interest.

Still, normal, normal, normal. Charlie reaches into his bag with a clammy hand he barely feels. Fingers brush the grained leather cover. And there they stop.

"Don't bother. You can't have many left."

Charlie has only one left.

"You should leave now."

Friendly, measured. Even and non-threatening. Like ordering a drink or telling a joke. Like reading aloud a transcript of what a calm conversation should sound like.

But the threat is there just the same.

"I called the cops the moment you came through the door. You can still go."

The tone is still friendly. The eyes, those eyes are something else.

"But you should go now."

13.

The van is off-white and featureless, the kind of thing driven by villains in made-for-TV movies in the '80s. The tires lope along sounding flat or the road is ridged like a cobblestone highway. The culprit means nothing to Charlie. They are all just outside sounds, so far removed from the lucidity of the ones in here with him.

The puppeteer was in the van when they picked up Charlie. He says he was hitching but Charlie doesn't know that this is true. He carries the air of a man who lies about anything he wants just because he likes the order of the words, not the content of the conversation. He looks tired when he thinks no one is looking.

The handcuff on his right wrist is tight enough to dig into the skin. The chain is short and the briefcase it connects to is black steel. His shoulders are thin. That case must double his weight but he carries himself with an undaunted self-possession. He sits on the wheel well and doesn't lift it and maybe he can't.

The driver looks back every few minutes with nervous glances but doesn't talk to Charlie. He's some kid, shaggy hair, dirty clothes, on his way to mom's or sister's or who-fucking-ever's, but something isn't right in his world and maybe that something is the passengers in back. Charlie and the puppeteer.

It's too late not to have stopped now, kid. It's too late to take it back.

"He's made of wood, you know."

The puppeteer has small eyes and rosy cheeks. He isn't wearing glasses but he looks like someone who should. Like a key piece of his features is missing. A cliché gone wrong, unfinished.

"Who?"

He pats his left hand against the steel box chained to the right. A gentle smile and drooped lids.

"His name is Fred."

There is a keypad on the lock of the case. Sophisticated and not cheap.

"What does Fred do?"

He looks at Charlie like there is something absurd about this and only this. He looks at Charlie like some part of his core is offended by this obscene stupidity.

"Nothing. He's made of wood."

———

A church bus and a '40s Ford truck and a ghetto taxi and after that Charlie is walking. He's said maybe a dozen words to any one of the drivers and no one seemed bothered by the quiet. Each does not look back as he or she drives away.

One streetlight blinks on in the fading light of day. What he walks up on, this is no town. One streetlight blinks on because there is only one streetlight visible for miles. A supermarket sits back from the highway as if it fell off the back of a truck and no one bothered to pull over to pick it up. The parking lot is almost empty but not quite. The lights are on inside the market but Charlie does not enter. No cars appear from any direction and there is no sound but the wind making senseless circuits from one side of the earth to the other and back again.

"Hello again."

Thick bristles of mustache hide his mouth but Charlie knows the man smiles anyway. The man sits on a concrete lip with arms hanging over knees. His tie has been lost somewhere along the way and the bottle in his hand is hidden in a bag and it is not Maalox but otherwise he hasn't changed a bit. His voice is accented, the kind of voice someone uses when they're hiding another accent with one that sounds American but is not. Like he's swallowing his vowels with overachieving consonants.

"How did your car's story end?"

Charlie doesn't think he himself is going to answer until his shoulders shrug and answer for him.

"That'll happen," says the man.

He takes a drink from the bottle that is not Maalox and looks out at a highway that runs on forever. Charlie sits down on the concrete next to him and stares out at that same world but surely, surely the worlds they are seeing are not the same.

"Where you from?" asks the man without turning.

Charlie looks over his own shoulder at the sun disappearing a little at a time behind the curve of the earth. He points the opposite direction. The man doesn't nod, doesn't acknowledge the answer or even his own question.

"What do you keep in that bag?"

Charlie hefts it with one hand like he's not sure what bag the man means.

"Just some work. It's almost over, anyway."

Maybe this is a lie but that's okay. This time the man does nod. He nods and he raises his own bag.

"Me too."

He drinks from what is hidden inside the brown paper covering. He drinks deeply and sets the bag down as he leans back to dig in the hip pocket of his slacks.

"You smoke?"

Charlie shakes his head and the man brings out a bent pack of cheap cigarettes, a brand Charlie has seen but not one he knows. The man shakes one out and lights it and shakes out another. He holds it out to Charlie and ignores the wagging rebuttal until Charlie's hand stops refusing and takes the cigarette. The man hands Charlie his lighter and lets his eyes go back to the highway, back to the east, back to the world and he exhales smoke as Charlie lights.

"You should start. You have to live for something."

Charlie doesn't hand back the lighter, sets it on the pavement and stares out at that same world. He sees what he sees and he watches it for a long time. Maybe he smokes the cigarette and takes another. Maybe he smokes that one too. Maybe they smoke the whole pack as the sun burns away to nothing behind their backs. No car passes in all this time and that is just fine. Everything is just fine.

Eventually the man stubs out no more than the filter of an old and spent cigarette nub and still looking out at that world he exhales a last heady breath of smoke.

"So where you headed?"

Charlie says nothing at all.

———

Car pulls to the shoulder at the last second, driver throws it in reverse and backs the diminutive piece of shined and overpriced hotrod up until he's parked only a car length in front of Charlie. Charlie keeps walking past as the window slides down. The car has to pull forward to catch up.

"I can take you a few miles up the road."

Charlie does not turn his head and he speaks only sparingly.

"How many miles?"

The car rolls forward, a foot on the brake. Brakes squeal. They need work.

"A few. Get in. I could use the company."

Something isn't right but Charlie gets in anyway. The man tips the panama that covers the greasy, uncut hair hanging past ears and back down neck to the collar of a suit that was once cream but looks sweated and slept-in for several unclean decades until the color has gone a murky, almost yellow tan. He wears wraparound shades like everyone else these dark future days.

He drives fast with one hand on the wheel and the other on the gearshift but the car is an automatic. His shoes are sporty and canvas and do not match his suit. He doesn't seem interested in Charlie's presence but speaks to fill the air with something.

"You're a long way from home, yeah?"

The phone in Charlie's bag begins to hum its forgotten tune and the man driving laughs wanton guffaws. Some unseen obstacle jumps into the roadway and he swerves to miss this phantom with the smooth transition of a professional. A minor bump as one tire touches grassy median and the glove compartment pops open to hit Charlie's knees. There are no gloves in the box but only a thick black book. A small gold lock with a small round keyhole. Little girl's diary-esque. The lock is broken and flaps with arrogance. Charlie looks at the man and the man looks at the road and the road only goes on ignoring it all at loathsome speeds.

The book is heavy in Charlie's hands, misleading weight and a smell like old forest floor, wet and untouched by light in years. Charlie opens to a page at random and his gaze wanders in silence across words scrawled in a delicate hand:

What I at first believed to be my Gift is only now revealed as Punishment Unending. To bear witness for a time is just, but to bear witness with no means to prevent and never a chance to change is a wickedness beyond human design. Only a God could ask such a thing of Man, to drive that knife so deep and still use method so convincingly banal as to shade this in a mask of righteousness.

"Is this your journal?"

He takes the little black book with the broken lock out of Charlie's hand and tosses it with casual disregard into the glove box.

"It's just a log. Clerical reportings. I keep the books for a major company. You've probably seen some of my work."

He turns his head for a moment and pushes the panama up on his brow. A slight shake, a negation of something key and then he's back facing the road.

"This is where you get out."

A town limits sign is coming up but has yet to reach their presence. The actual town is still miles off.

"Can't you drop me off in town?"

He pulls to a full stop and looks at Charlie once more. "No."

———

The tiny subcompact with the dented doors and fender and hood and the spray-painted doodles running up its sides pulls up after only a few minutes of Charlie watching faceless cars with empty passengers pass along on the road to nowhere. Charlie does not think twice as he runs around to the other side and open the door.

A wild man with shaky mad eyes looks out of the passenger seat.

Charlie squeezes into the back seat and moves over until those mad eyes cannot any longer see him in the mirror.

"You stole my car."

It sounds childish and petty and still it is nothing but true. The pale boy in the driver's seat wipes his nose on the sleeve of the black hooded sweatshirt he wears and shakes his head slowly back and forth. Charlie does not think this is a denial of stealing the car. Maybe a denial that it ever was his car to steal.

The wild man with the mad eyes looks around at everything and nothing and mumbles incoherent triflings to himself.

"I still need it a little longer," adds Charlie with some petulance.

The pale boy blinks and sweat stands out on his forehead, blood runs from his nose and his eyelids dip a little as he weaves on the road but never slips over the line.

"You need to pull over."

The wild man growls and Charlie grips the seats and the boy coughs and gags and blood stands out in the lines at the corner of his mouth and the car slows as his foot falls from the gas but it doesn't stop, only drifts.

"Pull over. Now."

Pink eyes open wide but he does not move to push the brake or even give notice of understanding. His hands slowly wander down the steering wheel until they fall from it altogether and those wide pink eyes beg for help in the mirror but there is no one here to give the kind of salvation he needs. The wild man reaches for the wheel but misses this and grabs the pale boy's wallet before opening a ragged mouth with more holes than teeth and letting out a shriek of animal triumph as he bails from the now-open door of the moving car to disappear into the night.

That ogre screech seems to keep pace with the car for a time. Even as Charlie climbs over the seat and presses into the gas it seems to be just outside far after it should be outrun.

Eventually it does fall away into the night, and this is somehow more horrible.

———

It can't still be night. It has been night for days. It cannot still be night but the sun has yet to come up and so Charlie can only wait and believe that day is out there somewhere.

He doesn't like stopping for hitchers. It's not safe. Not in this day and age. There was a brief point in history when Man went from being a beast with a cudgel to a creampuff in spectacles, when nature relaxed with a toddy after work and kicked off its shoes to watch the roar of a fire in a fireplace while listening to a trite but involved radio broadcast play out a serial drama, and this was maybe good enough. For the time, for that beast, maybe this was good enough. That day has gone, that brief liaise with gentility a mere sweet night's loving and now that night has slipped away and Man has come to the dawn of a new day in which he sees the true nature of the species sneaking back to the forefront to rape and pillage and cast off the veil of implied civilization as it gnaws with interest on the meaty flesh of its first morning's kill.

This is why Charlie does not like stopping for hitchers.

Miles from town. Any town. He slows and stops and he looks in the back seat. The pale boy is sleeping stretched across the seat with his arms folded across his chest. Charlie's bag is under the boy's head, lumpy but he doesn't seem bothered. The bleeding has stopped but there is a thick, unhealthy wetness to his breathing.

The man who steps up to the passenger door does not at first lean down. Stands with a torso visible and one fist held out clutching a handful of ribbons that drift up above Charlie's vision. Window comes down and the man's other hand comes up to rest there. A wad of green straw hair hangs from that hand like the scalp of a dead alien. The fingers of that hand come up to hold the scalp out for Charlie like a gift or some horror offering before falling again to their perch on the window's sill. The other hand holding the ribbons comes down beside it and there he leans, holding, waiting.

Charlie looks into the back seat once more but the kid has not stirred.

The man belonging to the hands doesn't so much lean into the window as ride a slow train down to eye level. A frilly yellow shirt with white and green polka dots hangs unbuttoned over a fat, hairy old-man belly. Scars run through that hair like territorial demarcations and one misshapen nipple sneaks out as he dips ever further into frame. Above is a wrinkled neck with wads of skin left over for when he runs low. Smeared yellow, not white, but yellow makeup runs down this neck to cake in the folds made by all that extra old-man flesh. And the chin, this comes into view leisurely, almost absently and then the mouth, detached, not smiling, not doing much of anything, all the more horrible next to the pained red smile drawn over this

mouth and stretching up yellow cheeks and past eyes cir-
cled in a purple so dark it could be a void with eyes looking
out.

That blank mouth opens and so does the red smiling
one that fills the mind with a blank hysteria and somehow
that gaping wound of a mouth finds a way to make words
come out to find Charlie waiting.

"Thank God you came along," says the painted man.

———

He watches. As Charlie drives the painted man
watches him and nothing else. The balloons attached to
the ribbons in that hand float around in the back seat
above the sleeping pale boy. Some of them have foil words
on them, cheery things like *HAPPY BIRTHDAY, JESSIE!*
or *GET WELL SOON!* and some have nothing at all. Half
a dozen total at least. Maybe twice that. They seem to
dance away when Charlie tries to count. It's better not to
look.

His hair is gray and his face is wrinkled, the makeup
caught in the lines of his life. There is a pink circle of untouched flesh where the wig still clutched in hand once sat.
His staring at Charlie is accented by Charlie's refusal to
look his direction.

It is a long time before he speaks.

"Why did you stop for me?"

Charlie watches the road. It does just as it should.

"Do you stop for hitchhikers often?"

Maybe Charlie shakes his head but this is no real answer. The lump in the back seat shifts and makes a noise
but does not wake up.

"Do you know who I am?"

"You're a clown."

"I'm a doctor."

He stirs and the balloons move in the back seat. He takes off his seatbelt.

"You haven't seen me on TV?"

He lets go the green scalp and reaches into a polka dot pocket.

"I'm very famous, you know. Whole worlds have heard of me."

The next few seconds fall all over themselves. The hand in the pocket happens first, slowly creeping out with a trim slip of metal held within. The object only begins to peek but does not make it all the way out. Next is the click from the back seat. Just a click of metal, something like the hammer of a pistol cocking back and a wet breathing voice speaking quietly.

"I think you should pull over," says the pale boy. "This man needs to get out."

There is an embarrassing moment that passes between everyone in the car and then Charlie is slowing and stopping and the clown looks with that blank expression hidden in fading yellow and then he is out the door and gone. The car is moving again when Charlie turns to look at the wheezing pale sick thing dying in the back seat.

"I didn't know you had a gun."

He sneezes blood into his sleeve and says nothing.

14.

It's easy to fall in line with the caravan. They trundle along like a line of elephants slowly winding toward some distant water hole just off the highway. From morning to midday no one stops. Curious eyes lean out from time to time to watch in the side mirror the strange car trailing behind, Charlie behind the wheel. Charlie mocks tugging at an air horn every time. The caravan drivers never honk.

Truck stop ends the trek. Greasy spoon stuck halfway between two distant somewheres. They circle the wagons and Charlie parks alongside like he belongs. Dozens dismount and stand around smoking. A handful head inside and so does Charlie.

Blast of conversation washes in waves as he comes through the door. Discussions of lives past and future in a symphony of voices, all these familiar faces haunted by memories and knocked over by thoughts. Laughing some, solemn others. A slow and awkward step past the checkerboard face of a tattooed man. His own gaze of un-aimed spite follows Charlie by.

Several large men with small thumbs and no necks sit at their own table drinking strong coffee. An earnest and pleasant smile greets Charlie as he sits. Perfect stranger but the man seems wholly at ease with this newcomer to his world. The other two sip coffee and show teeth and sip again. This one nods like Charlie asked a question.

"Thinking of joining up?"

Charlie doesn't answer at first, not because he doesn't understand the question but because it honestly hadn't occurred to him that this is an option until just this moment.

And then he does.

"Just crossing paths for a bit."

A woman with a pen in one hand and a bottle of ketchup in the other stops beside the table. She writes something on a pad she balances on the ketchup arm and trades rehearsed lines with the two toothy brutes.

"A friend of mine might stay," Charlie offers some time later.

"We'll take your sickly albino. Why not."

Charlie takes a drink of bottled water. The smiling gent with shoulders threatening to swallow his head nods as food arrives. He smiles at the woman with the food and nods again. He seems pleased with everything existence has to say about this day.

"A few of the crew have been asking about you."

Charlie shakes his head to clear whatever this begins to mean to him.

"Well, you made an impression on somebody," says the   man.

A small plate like an exaggerated tea saucer is set in front of Charlie by a passing wraith. Toasted bread and nothing more. He eats slowly, tiny bites, savoring each with wells of will. He speaks between bites.

"Where are you going from here?"

The man eats from a plate heaped with eggs and bacon and toast and potatoes. Coffee and orange juice and water, a line of glasses set up around the plate's edge like a wall of troops guarding some wondrous treasure.

"We're setting up at the fairgrounds. We'll be in town for a week."

Charlie's sigh is unexpected.

"I can't stay a week."

"I didn't think you could."

The man looks at his food as he says more.

"Someone wants to see you before you go."

"Who?"

The man shrugs. Charlie trudges on.

"I have time. Let me sleep. Let me sleep today and tomorrow I'll see them."

Charlie has to take a drink before he goes on. And another. Half the bottle is gone before the question will come out.

"What do they want?"

Looks up from his food. Smiles and happy and the world is everything it should be.

"Don't be a fool. Nobody knows what they want."

———

The clock is in the shape of a cat. Its eyes look to the right and they do not move at all, staring with empty patience and unending resolve at the wreckage of Charlie's guilty soul. The room is cold and it is dark and even the lights shining from poles outside or the shouting voices of men working to raise this carnival from the ground do nothing to penetrate this place. The cat would be watching Charlie sleep but he only sits here with blankets pulled to neck and body wrapped around itself, his eyes staring back at those of the cat clock.

Full-length closet, unreasonably deep for an alcove tucked into the side of a bus. Charlie watches the dark corners of the room with only passing interest. It is the closet that takes hold of his mind and laughs when he begs it to let go. The closet door, that thin piece of corkboard

painted to look like a stronger material, something, anything that could keep the monsters out.

That thin closet door stands open.

The weight on the corner of the bed is what forces his
eyes closed. There is nothing there and this is what he repeats ad nauseam with every ounce of being. Nothing
there and nothing there. The room grows colder and there
is nothing there. The voices outside dampen to a whisper
and there is nothing there. There is nothing there and
there is nothing there.

It shifts its weight and speaks. Its voice is patient. It has
waited lifetimes.

"Where are you going, Charlie?"

———

The darkness outside is bashed to bloody fragments by
the floodlights strapped to poles crisscrossing the grounds
where the construction goes on at full force. Charlie stands
in the doorway of the bus for a long time looking out and
sipping at the remains of coffee left in a pot by who knows
who. A cracked voice older than its years tries to speak and
fails. Charlie turns and moves to the little table nearby. He
clears his throat and that old voice speaks again.

"Couldn't sleep?"

The coffee is cold and awful but it holds him in the moment and he drinks of it deeply.

"Bad dreams."

The man sits at the little table taking this in. His skin is
a sickly color, something yellowing but more than that,
veins and bone showing through, that translucent flesh
showing off more than those cold eyes ever could. Strange

eyes, a deep sadness and a well of knowing and something more all swirling in an embrace so horrible it hurts to look at. His left hand strokes across the cover of a battered green folder set before him on the table. His right sits motionless, folded across his chest in somber repose. Already halfway to the grave.

"How bad?"

"I've had this one before."

He eyes Charlie for a long time. His eyes don't look at Charlie's hands, they crawl over them with an uneasy hunger that makes Charlie uncomfortable. A vampiric thirst for some part of his soul accessed in the lines of the hands he will not be forced to put out before the skeletal specter tearing him apart with its sickening eyes.

"You know I can't help you," says the man.

Sip and warm fake smile. There is no sleep in Charlie's voice as he responds.

"I don't know any such thing."

The man shrugs. Neither man believes it matters. It doesn't.

"There was a girl here before," says Charlie "She's not here anymore."

"I need to see her."

He waits for more. He knows Charlie will speak first.

"Will she come back?"

"What is she to you?"

The man's dry pause is not for dramatic effect but it might as well be. Charlie's heart jumps and doesn't slow and he doesn't understand this. He tries to but he just doesn't.

"You can't save anybody, Charlie."

Charlie opens his bag and reaches inside with one hand. That hand stays there holding onto what's inside for a long time. There is something solemn in this moment, something he could never explain in all the time he has left, something about random broken hearts and lost strangers unsaved and that forlorn spasm that yanks a person's insides when they try to imagine their own death not in words but in that spinning loss of even the most flimsy grounding to a kind of existence, not the feeling of going but of not ever being. It is a momentary touch of something deep in Charlie that he pushes away but he cannot deny its presence was there for one unbearable instant. It's something like losing faith or finding faith or missing something expected to lose or never expected to find at all. A sense of loss completely misunderstood.

Awful.

In a sudden motion Charlie pulls his hand from the bag and lays a large stack of bills on the table. Unbound U.S. currency of all denominations in a neat but erratic stack pushed across until it almost but not quite touches the edge of that green notebook.

"Give her this. Make sure she gets it. Make sure she's—"

The word is *okay* but he doesn't know why. He doesn't know what it answers or what it speaks to, he doesn't know what it solves or what demon it devours.

"Anyway," says Charlie, unable to finish the thought.

Those terrible eyes look up at Charlie as he stands and nods an acknowledgment of something private and futile. That voice thick with an age this sickly young man hasn't lived speaks up as Charlie moves to escape.

"Sometimes its hard knowing who the villain is, isn't it."

15.

The highway peels away at an obscene gait. The engine first knocks and then sputters and finally screams a sound of metal and fire and the death throes of a gentle steel beast not meant to live such a hard life. It carries on far beyond what can be reasonably expected of it but eventually the seizures of its dying moments end and what is left is just that death and nothing else.

It is only then that the highway ceases its leaping gallop. It is only then that the world stands still.

———

Hardpan causeway cut or packed into field from years of use. Charlie follows too long as the highway begins to veer off to its own whimsy and the trail continues on. The grass lengthens and envelops and soon his knuckles brush along its ceiling as he moves. Soft and light and waving in the breeze. He closes his eyes and is carried onward, arms outstretched, fingers playing over grass with the most delicate touch and that hard ground under feet and nothing else in all imagination holding him to this world.

"Watch your step."

His eyes fall on a thin boy sitting on a rock outcropping in what must once have been a stream. Clay shell of its former glory carves a path through the grassland and weaves away to hide somewhere beyond. The boy looks up at the sun and squints. His skin is darkened from days in the sun. He cannot be more than thirteen but his voice is soft and ageless. Here and there pools remain in the streambed, some no more than a thin sheen in the dirt, others black and infinite.

"You could fall in and never come out."

Charlie nods and he does watch his step. He hefts his bag and all its weight and sets it laboriously in front of him on the ground, a small grunt escaping as he does. The boy holds a fishing pole in front of him, the line disappearing into one of those dark pools. He reels in the line but there is nothing on the end. His hands are filthy.

"It's a long walk out here. You must be thirsty."

Charlie shakes his head and the boy offers nothing. Charlie opens the bag and takes out a bottle. He drinks from it and puts it back. The boy doesn't look his way until the bag is closed. The boy's feet are shoeless. There are no footprints in any direction but the ones behind Charlie and one muddy smear on the rock below the boy's perch, as if he has always been in just this spot.

"Not everyone can be saved."

Charlie says nothing.

"Have you learned anything?"

Charlie shakes his head. The boy's hair is short but hasn't been cut in some time. He runs a hand through it and looks again at the sun. He closes his eyes and feels the breeze. Charlie starts to do the same but hesitates, then doesn't do it at all. He picks up the bag and moves further into the swath cut by the dead stream. He looks in the direction of the highway and the path at his back. He looks to the course the hardpan follows and the swaying grass around it. He looks to its kinks and the path twisting back to where the highway lies with all its indifferent compass points. Charlie looks around once more.

He should say something and he knows it. There is a time for an offering and it is now. He should give something but he has nothing left to give.

"It's okay," says the boy with a sad smile. He looks back to his fishing pole, to the line dangling lazily atop an oversized black puddle. Charlie stands there as time moves on, but the boy says no more and soon Charlie's feet are carrying him once more.

16.

The window set into the wall of the one-room shack built at the turn of a century no longer animate is caked thick with the dust of infinite empty miles. Tracks of a train not present trail forward and back and there is no curve to them and nothing resembling an end. A rusting silo with a tower and catwalk far above sit dead and impotent in the distance. A fallen ladder lays on the ground nearby. The fields in every direction grow nothing but rock and hard, unfilled nothing.

Tar, hot and melted in the boiling day, clings to the soles of Charlie's dusty, broken shoes as he leaves the tracks behind.

"Train ticket," and, "please."

Eyes set deep in fat round cheeks soaked red with sun and a lifetime of wear. Wire-rimmed bifocals rest on a thin bone of nose. Pupils turn at the sound of Charlie's voice. Stubs of fingers on a fat round hand push the cloudy window aside with a noisy rattle of glass and frame. He speaks with a croak of voice not used in ages.

"No train. Bus."

One of those bulbous tomato hands reaches up to put a pen cap between swollen lips. He works flat worn teeth over the cap, idly chewing as pupils sneak in slow circles to take in Charlie's unmoving incidence. There is no pen in sight.

"I need to take the train," says Charlie.

Jaws clench on the cap's plastic face, rolling and clenching, creating a continent of textures. Squeak of metal as a child rides along beside the tracks on a small bicycle. Training wheels poke from the sides, one longer than the other, leaving the bike leaning to one side. Tiny and grim, this wraith could be a boy or a girl or it could be a ghost imagined in the miles of nowhere. The child stops and the bike leans and this dusty misanthrope turns a sun-tattered face to look Charlie's way. Charlie turns back to the round face in the window as the man speaks in guttural tongues.

"Station in town. Next bus'll get ya there."

A high wind blows from the west and dust sprays the building with angry fists. Charlie squints and a whistle screams hollow frustrations at the world.

"When's the next bus come through?"

Two fingers take pen cap from mouth. A line of spit follows slow between, growing and hanging like a clothes-line between hand and face, drooping until it breaks under the weight of its own existence. Squeak of wheels and Charlie doesn't turn until the sound is far away, and even then he turns only eyes, not face, and he sees nothing but dust blowing over old tracks for miles. The round face with the spectacles cracks open with a grisly rictus of perverse joy.

"Any time."

———

Charlie sits on a bench and the world moves slowly on toward wherever it wants to go. Brakes shriek and a behemoth stops and Charlie gets onboard and he sits on another bench. A sign says the name of a city far off and he stares at it as it blinks the name in slow repetition. Strangers face forward and don't look at each other. A small man in a dirty shirt eats dry cereal from a torn box. Grime sullies the face of an older man with hard, square shoulders. Blood is caked under one nostril and he breathes long breaths while he looks out the window. There is no sound but the wind and the tinny murmur of a young woman's earphones, tiny buds attached with wires that run down a collar and through a sleeve and into nowhere. She wears a fur-lined coat several sizes too large. The weather is warm and getting hot but she seems not to notice. The bus drives a sane speed and never, ever slows down.

———

Blank stares pass at lackadaisical paces as careful hands hold onto a polished railing leading off of the bus and into the world. Exhaust and the offbeat rattle of machine chugging bounces off walls in the roofed tin shed that houses the depot. Huge and old, once a hangar years ago. Charlie stands on a platform as swarms bustle about. A kid with a guitar tied to his back but no case hands him a hand-rolled cigarette. Charlie nods thanks but the kid has already turned away. Charlie has no lighter so he only holds it awkwardly between two fingers until he passes it on to an old man hiding in an ocean of wrinkles and he looks for a sign of where he should go.

Eventually he finds it.

A coffee shop hangs attached to the small depot, a shed with a bar and the rich bitter scent of better times. People come and go and some chat with the fresh faces who serve the sweet beverages with colorful names while others take their drinks and only nod at the outbursts of friendliness offered up by these intense baristas. Charlie takes a seat at the bar. He dials the office number but hangs up and dials Jess instead. He hangs up before anyone answers. He sets down the phone and can only sit staring, unsure. It rings. He picks up but doesn't talk. He waits, listening to words, questions asked with a lighthearted concern, but he does not relate to that lackadaisical tone and he no longer knows if he can express this feeling with material so fleeting as words. He hangs up. He has no idea what time it is.

The pale man in the long coat sits sipping black coffee from an impossibly small teacup. He sits in his place at the bar as if he has only ever been in just this place, sprouting casually from that seat from the beginning of time to its end.

"How are sales, charlatan?"

The bustle of railway traffic spins all about and for just a moment Charlie considers slipping away on the current of those shifting bodies, but the question grabs hold and he leans in to offer something like answer.

"Ever get the feeling you're in the wrong business?" asks Charlie.

The pale man sips his drink with a pinkie held out.

"Not ever," he says. "Second-guessing your place in the world?"

"I walk in and out of lives without ever touching them."

"You spread gospels when you want to be writing them."

Charlie nods. His smile is unashamed.

"I like that. Yeah."

An unpleasant snort of frank derision escapes the pale man as he stands.

"You're not special, charlatan."

He drops a dollar on the counter and taps it with one long finger. He winks at a barista who smiles and winks back.

The roar of the long black hardtop's engine coming to life in the train yard's adjacent lot shakes Charlie's hands as he fumbles with his tie. Numb hands adjust and fail, straighten again, but his efforts change nothing and the tie remains askew, turned from center, its knot an awkward bulb. A train whistle calls all boarders.

———

The train is sparsely populated with randomly spawned clichés from various eras of Americana. Charlie doesn't make eye contact as he looks for a seat. The places are numbered but he ignores this. A middle-aged man holds a yo-yo with the string unfurled at his feet and he looks with vacant eyes out a window as the train begins to rumble underfoot. The man says something to himself and his reflection smiles.

Charlie sits several rows from the nearest person.

Well-dressed women of a bitter vintage pass through the car looking for a dining car or just wandering. Charlie sits with his bag on the floor and his hands at his sides. The world speeds by outside, sand and rock and other things from time to time. A mountain and a sky. These things are always there but he cannot always see them. Sometimes he sees his reflection. Sometimes he sees nothing but night and these times he wonders if he should sleep but he doesn't. Sometimes there is a face.

Sometimes it isn't his own.

"Heading west, are we?"

Charlie didn't see the man sit down. A dozen empty seats nearby and he's too close, sharing the seat. He eats from a paper bag of peanuts, taking one and cracking the shell, eating one at a time and leaving the mess on the floor between his thick, scuffed boots. His hair is cropped short but hasn't been recently cut, is just beginning to get a disheveled look, a month or so out like a man on the run.

"That's the way the train is headed," says Charlie.

The man looks offended, an overachieving pout puffing up his features. He sits back in his seat and munches peanuts. His knees rest on the seat in front of him, feet dangling in air. Strings of shell lay on the belly of his black dress shirt.

"That it is. That it is. Do a lot of traveling, do ya?"

"I was a salesman in a past life."

"Were you, now?" he says, as Charlie pushes his bag aside with a foot. "What did you sell?"

"God. Mostly God."

Peanut grinding between crooked but clean teeth. Shells tossed to the floor without care.

"He's big. You must be loaded."

Maybe Charlie smiles, brief and full of sin.

"I do okay."

"So you're a believer in past lives then?"

Charlie offers nothing.

"I'm not much for past lives," says the man. "I'm pretty well stocked up on the current one."

Careful hands fold the lip of the paper bag and set it on the next seat. Ivory buttons are undone and black sleeves roll up to show hairless arms from wrist to elbow. A thick pink fault line of scar travels up from the space between the first finger and thumb of each hand all the way to the crook of elbow. He runs a finger over these as he tells his story in slow, even tones. The kind of voice that has all the time in the world.

"Fuck."

Charlie means to say it with more force, feels it come up from inside with more force, a plug of pressure behind the word but all that comes out is a wheeze and that one ineffectual syllable.

"You tell me you sold God? I think I met Him once."

He touches those scars with delicacy, the hard surface cut months ago or longer but he still runs the pads of his fingers across their carapace like it was their first time. He goes on. Charlie is no longer sure to whom the man is speaking.

"Not Him exactly, but something like it. I could see God in the eyes of the one who did all the heavy lifting. The one with the tattoos, he was just window dressing. A fast talker with snake oil to move and nothing but. But that other one, he was quiet while the first guy was reading the cards for me. He didn't say anything when Mr. Tattoo first looked at my hands or when he went back to his cards. It wasn't until all the bullshit went by that that other one moved his chair over and looked me in the face. The tattoo guy is forgotten by this point. That other one, he takes my hand and goes dead still. Just like that, all bullshit's gone. This guy, he runs his thumb over my hand, my palm, between every finger on one hand and then the other. And this whole time he's looking right in my face, and his other hand, it's running over the cover of this green notebook, light touches, like he's just reminding himself it's there, and he finally lets my hand go and says to me, 'You don't have to die.' Just like that. Like I'm supposed to know what that means. I take my hand back. It isn't until later I realize I was wiping my hands on my jeans ever since he touched me. Like whatever he had was catching."

His laugh isn't hysterical, but there are no words for what that laugh is.

"The tattooed guy dealt the cards but I could tell the moment I walked in it was the other one who read them."

Not talking to Charlie at all now. Quiet words, head turned down. Prayer.

"That one read my palms."

Finger wandering over scar. Relearning surface. Almost searching.

"It was bad news."

There is something terrible and intimate about this and Charlie has to look away. Silence is everywhere for a long time, the world outside the train a white blanket of meaningless humming and inside a disquieting stillness until he breaks through with a throaty breath and words like waking up.

"Tell me something."

In the look that passes through his face there is some kind of expectation. Charlie offers the only thing he finds to give.

"Charlie," says Charlie.

"Tell me something, Charlie. What is it you're out here looking for? What brings you here? To this point, here and now. This train. What is it that brings a man like you to such a place?"

Charlie thinks about his words. He looks at his own hands folded in his lap and he thinks. He looks at the man's hands doing much the same, the sleeves now rolled down to cover the miles of overextended lifeline that run down those arms. He thinks about the man's words. He looks at the reflected faces in the window of the train as some world unknown drifts by on the other side, that world with no interest in the answer or even the question. He answers in a whisper anyway. Just in case that world is listening.

"Life."

———

A new railcar.

"Of course I believe in ghosts."

Charlie takes a seat far away from the man but the man changes seats to sit closer to Charlie. Charlie looks over a shoulder but no one follows him back to this car. The happy man who sits down close to his seat rubs the palms of his hands together and he is the only person here.

"Wouldn't you? It only makes sense."

His hands are callused from years of work. Work. That's what he calls it. He laughs like it's a joke and he wipes the dirt from his hands but they remain unclean. A cloth bag hangs from his belt by a strip of oily gold string. A soft tinkle of metal when he moves. Something thicker inside. He touches it absently.

"I worked in so many cities. Rich cemeteries are private. Nice ones. The nice ones are the small ones."

He looks like no one in particular. Just some working schlub. He probably looks a lot like Charlie.

"The rich always want to take it with them."

It isn't a nervousness that Charlie sees in the man's face but the man's happy ease slips visibly.

"I probably would too."

He looks ashamed and somehow defiant. He looks Charlie in the face.

"I probably deserve it."

The change is there, something clear in his face, stark and afraid. He touches the pouch at his side but the look doesn't lessen. The fear claws deeply and without care.

"I didn't know!"

He probably begins to cry in slow, anguished sobs but Charlie stands and move away and does not slow. Before the door to the car slides before him he turns and asks just one question.

"Where does this train go?"

The gravedigger looks up but does not wipe the tears from his face. There is something terrible about this but he seems unaffected by his own humility. He only shrugs broken shoulders.

"I've always been on this train."

The sound and feel of the train slowing begins long before motion stops and Charlie begins to wonder if he's imagined it, if things are slowing at all and then the train has stopped. A man in a square hat looks his way as Charlie picks up his bag and holds it close. The man moves to the next car.

A window comes down. The air is filled with a thick smell like hot sweat that clings. Acres of empty concrete stand open on the other side of that window. No one has gotten off of the train. A fading hopscotch grid is drawn with a child's attention to detail but no numbers are filled in. A broken stone triangle sits in the first square, the edge of some long-lost work of engineering or a creation of natural design. Chalk and nothing more.

A man stands alone on the edge of the macadam, beyond him a field of grass. The smell of wet night on the air comes from that direction, something earthy and sane. He stands close to it with hands in pockets of a gray pullover. His face is turned slightly to the sky.

The clouds blow by in darkness. The smell of life is encroached by the smell of humanity, though there is none about. The man takes hands out of the pullover's pockets and puts them in the pockets of jeans. His eyes flick to the train just once, then back to the sky. He is still standing that way as the train begins to move once more.

———

He's slept for years and no face in the car is familiar. How many stops have passed is a mystery he spends almost no time considering. His bag is next to his leg. No one is near and the car is almost empty.

Outside the train is uninterested night. The lights inside are dim, just enough glow to hold inside the fragmentary images of all its meager inhabitants. The rumble of steel somewhere below has ceased and everything is still. Things do not move.

The man looking at Charlie isn't a man looking at Charlie. Sometimes he is the top of a hat seen over the lumpy stuffing of an itchy train car seat. Sometimes he is the sound of paper rattled as a page is turned. Sometimes he is these things still but something else underneath. Something worse. Sometimes he isn't there at all.

Charlie slides to the edge of his seat and the man is still there. He is still a man. Thick work boots caked with brown and gray dirt on bottoms and sides, yellow grass between hard rubber grips. Old pants, baggy and rough spun, the kind they used to make, pants that last lifetimes, generations. The top leg absently kicks, counting off every other second in a habitual twitch. Gloved hands hold a paper from weeks ago. The fingers of the cotton gloves are missing, loose threads hanging where they were torn. The nails are long and jagged, worn. The paper's front page shows a man Charlie has seen before but no one famous. The pages are yellowing at the edges. Every time he turns the page a faded black waistcoat appears wrapped around his frame. Brown sleeves protrude, their cuffs unbuttoned. Every time he turns the page his eyes come up to meet Charlie's, sly glances that almost go unnoticed. Cautious eyes, professional and mean. A hard face with insomniac bruising around those eyes, 1930s unkempt, a tan of dust on skin hard and thick. Unshaven for less than a week.

Bowler hat, lines of crease where someone grabbed it from a head with uncaring hands once upon a time.

Every time the goon turns the page his grin disappears.

Waking groan and the world heaves as the train comes to life. Charlie's bladder aches and he knows he is awake. He wonders if someone will take his seat when he is gone but there is no one to take it. He takes his bag and leaves the empty seat behind.

Drunken gait, the train gains speed as he walks. Moves faster and he bounces off of seatbacks. He nears and he slows. The face on the front page looks out at Charlie, at the world, a face full of crazy laughing at the world through a painted smile wholly pleased and unrepentant. The headline reads KILLER CLOWN CAUGHT! COPS LAUGH LAST! in small manic lettering.

The fingers shake the paper as they turn another page and the goon they belong to looks up with his own grin as Charlie passes.

"Damn thing," says the goon.

And it is. It is a damn thing.

———

Car after car has passed below his wandering feet for what must be hours in dogged search of an end but the train sprawls on far past the point at which it has any right to. Doors slide shut on silent treads as he rounds corners or passes slowly through empty halls. Countryside is night and day and night again and the world is not this big but the train never slows.

A film like rust but wet and veiny first crawls and then entombs the walls of the passages Charlie slips through on his way to what lies in front. He tries to outrun its malicious growth but as his steps tread faster the miasma only thickens and he becomes ensnared in this quicksand world of budding decay. The world outside the windows he passes is foreign only because he knows no other word for what he sees. He looks and his mind rejects and he looks away. It is no world a man would wish to imagine and none that could be looked upon with anything approaching sanity.

A whistle releases a banshee howl that scrapes away the lucid layers of the mind. The infant imagination underneath understands this subhuman sound not at all but accepts it with the immediacy of the truly unbiased. Doors don't slide shut anymore because there are no more doors here, only an endless yawning maw that Charlie has no choice but to plod through.

The smell of smoke and burn fills lungs with every heated breath. Nostrils sting and eyes water and the smell turns stomach. Fire and flesh and coal and ruin. A furnace filled with all hell boils the veins of this savage steel snake with only rage, only rage.

A whistle releases a banshee howl and the train never slows.

———

The two orbs of light before the oncoming locomotive meet not in a lover's embrace but in the mad tangle of an angry back-alley fuck. What they illuminate does not matter. There is nothing alive in this world.

Fire drips in irresponsible patters from tallow draped over skull of the thing looking out at Charlie in the window's reflection. Its eyes are sunken and only barely defined in the bruised pools of their sockets. A low, insane pseudo-intelligence runs screaming in and out of them at will, glitters of a knowing intellect only distant shimmers in the darkness of their frenzied world.

The slick leather of veined wings unfurl at its back but do not open to their full unknowable span, only roll to the ground like a cloak made of skin. An oversized vinyl chair hides the thing's back, the iron pole poking out from the bottom of the chair bolted to the dense iron floor with huge plugs of the same dark metal.

Long fingers ending not in nubs of soft pink flesh but hard yellow bone talons cling with fury and strength to gears protruding from a simple panel set under the wide front window. The right jams a lever as hard as it can push forward, the globe at the top of the stick threatening to break off. The left only sits there, shaking as it grips white-knuckle hard around a handle that connects two long, slender pieces to the panel beneath.

Charlie stands in what he hopes is silence but a thin wheeze escapes his throat anyway as he wants to scream, opens his mouth to scream, is going to scream. His hands fumble with the latch on his bag and then fumble inside and he does not know what he is grabbing and then he does know and it is a vain kind of hope but it is there and that is all that he has and his breath comes again and there is no scream to come with it. Maybe tears streak down a tired face or maybe that is just another nightmare, not worth notice.

"Hep you?" says a friendly voice, accented as the man it belongs to turns around and away from a bright white instrument panel filled with all manner of gadgets and meters and knobs and keys and he looks at Charlie. A toothless gold-rush prospector lilt, the kind of voice no one really has. This man is not toothless and he is not a prospector, only a little thin and a little strange to look upon with his bright red hair and face tall and only just too tight. His hands fold in his lap, long and thin and swollen at joints. He smiles a wide smile like all the world is in on the joke, and maybe it is. Maybe it is.

Craig Rodgers has published several books and intends to publish a few more before he fakes his own death.

Also by Craig Rodgers

The Ghost of Mile 43
Moonbeams
Twenty Ponds
One More Number
Francis Top's Grand Design

Collect Them All!

The Sun Still Shines on a Dog's Ass, *The War on Xmas*, and *Mere Malarkey* by Alan Good

Drift, *The Ghost of Mile 43*, *One More Number*, and *Francis Top's Grand Design* by Craig Rodgers

Consumption and Other Vices by Tyler Dempsey

Coming in February 2024:
Awful People by Scott Mitchel May

DEATHOFPRINT.PRESS